GHOST TOWN

THE WHITEROCK INCIDENT PART 2

RAW TROOPS

LEIF J. ERICKSON

TABLE OF CONTENT

UNITED STATES OF AMERICA

ISBN: 978-0-9907025-0-4

Confidential Report:

File Number 'WR0020130715-Main'

Ground Reconnaissance at the

Whiterock Incident

After the first Ghost Town Event, during the time now designated "The Whiterock Incident" as documented by FBI Agent Ethan Drew's journal and notes, a panel within the Domestic Terrorism branch of the FBI began to put together a rescue plan. The situation was allowed to play its course while containment procedures were put into place. Dr. Victor Tesla's intentions were made clear, and we have double confirmation that he has taken Ghost Town Labs private. Dr. Tesla had put together a board of directors who are running the company while he and his team handle the science.

The issue of Ghost Town Labs being private poses two distinct and unique problems. First, the United States government must be in control of the mind control systems and the machines used to create the ghosts. In the wrong hands, these devices used could spell the end of humanity. The second problem: Ghost Town Labs has patients and licensing agreements for many products that are being used every day—translation, a multi-million dollar per year revenue stream that has been taken away.

The goal has now become total destruction of the current Ghost Town Labs structure. A new company has been formed within the government, Quad Force. They will handle all the issues that Ghost Town Labs was dealing with, and it will be staffed with all new personnel. We must find Dr. Tesla before he unleashes the machine on a highly populated area. Dr. Tesla, by order of the President of the United States is to be found and questioned. All other team members are to be killed on sight and their bodies burned. This includes any and all of the women in his army who've been through the mind control programs.

Other orders moving forward include finding and apprehending Ethan Drew, Michelle Tesla, and Madison Tesla, all of whom have not been seen or heard from since they left New Church upon Ethan finishing his journal. Other persons that must be found are Hannah Jones, Mackenzie Hanson, and Anna Jenson, all who disappeared after dropping other Whiterock survivors off before returning to extract Ethan,

Michelle, and Madison. These six must be questioned to see what other information they have.

The only information we know outside of Ethan's report is that all the townsfolk of Whiterock were turned into ghosts; they are still roaming the forest. Ethan reported that the Ghost Town Labs women shot the people being loaded onto our buses. It's now apparent that there was a devise running that turned the dead into ghosts as the women shot them. The women then destroyed the people who were already ghosts, but we have no information as to why they did that. This horrifying information came to us by satellite imaging and it showed how quickly the machine can turn people.

To carry out these orders, an elite group of soldiers have been selected. RAW Troops, or Remote Alert Warriors, was formed as a unit five years ago when we got the first reports of Dr. Tesla's possible betrayal. A RAW troop's team is a full squad that breaks down into small groups of between two and six members. Each small unit has a spot commander that has all the orders and runs the unit whiles the Tactical Commander, or TC, runs the entire squad.

RAW troops differ from most military command groups in that only the TC wears black military fatigues while the rest of the troops will be outfitted to blend in with the local populace. RAW troops have trained with special guns called E.P.D. guns, or electro-plasma distorters that are the only way to disperse the ghosts that now inhabit Whiterock. All RAW troops conceal a normal Beretta 92FS 9mm handgun as well. One RAW troop, a fencing and knives expert, carries a sword and throwing knives made of the E.P.D. material.

The RAW troops have prepared for this situation. This is why they were created. Every RAW troop is lethal at hand-to-hand combat and has received black belts in at least three different martial arts. They are the most disciplined members of the military and all are of the highest intelligence. We have selected the best of the RAW troops for this first mission: the investigation of Whiterock and the surrounding area.

The troops will arrive at their locations and they will get their first taste of combat with the ghosts. They are scheduled to arrive in the morning, three days after Ethan left the journal on the altar of New Church. They will hold at their location with instructions to kill or destroy anything that's hostile, until dusk. At that time, they are all to converge on either the Tesla farm, or the elevator at Blackstone Hollow where they will enter the lab, destroy all threats, and gather information about where Dr. Tesla may have gone.

A new tactical commander will be flown in by helicopter to enter the lab. The chopper will be under orders to take any survivors of the Whiterock Incident to safety. The chopper flying over the area will be the signal to the teams to get to the farm or the elevator, and the chopper leaving the area is the signal to enter the labs. Any force needed has been authorized to enter the labs. Once the team has investigated the lab and is out of the area, a grouping of military planes will fly over the area, dropping napalm to burn the forest, destroying the rest of the ghosts with fire. The only luck we've had with this situation is that the ghosts haven't left the forest. We are not sure why, but speculate that they cannot travel far from the point where they were turned.

Confidential Report:

File Number 'WR0020130715-Main'

Ground Reconnaissance at the

Whiterock Incident

-Amendment-

This report is compiled from the teams who searched the area. The report is the first hand accounts of the surviving members of the RAW troops as verified by our satellite surveillance. While we knew that causalities would be inevitable, we were not expecting losses in the numbers that we received. One high-level trainer thought it wise not to inform all the members of what they would actually be fighting as he thought that they wouldn't believe and then not take the training seriously. As the teams enter the area, only the spot commanders and the tactical commander knew what they were up against. That proved to be a fatal mistake...

Chapter #1

Beta Watch Team

The scorching sun was high in the midday sky as the temperature hovered at slightly over one hundred degrees with a high humidity. Jake Wright wiped the sweat from his brow and sighed, knowing he had a long time left standing out in the sweltering heat. A massive man, standing six feet, four inches tall and built like a linebacker, Jake couldn't help but laugh at the thought of all the training that he'd had in the RAW program and that their first mission was in the tiny farming town of Whiterock.

With no real information about this mission given to the troops, Jake tightened his grip on his EPD shotgun. Jake thought it looked like an ordinary twelve gauge shotgun, but he felt the ammunition they used in it was too light. He had a pistol of the same design along with his regular pistol. Jake paced, worried that they hadn't heard from any other unit since they were dropped off at the old forest road that morning. Jake and his unit were to man the roadblock and destroy any threats. Jake wished he could use his training for more than guarding a road.

Jake gazed down the main crossroad. He'd been there all day and had not seen one car. He thought that was odd considering how rushed the team was in getting to the area. Jake figured that they were going to be set down in a hot zone and there would be bullets flying the second they hit the ground. However, he and the other members of the Beta Watch team just paced back and forth, looking at a deserted highway going through the forest.

Jake looked at his team members. He didn't know either of them personally, but he knew they were in the top of their class. First was Blake Otto, a tall and lanky man, with stringy blonde surfer hair and a very narrow face. Blake was the fastest runner in all of the RAW troops, and he'd even raced in the Olympics. Blake held the RAW records for both short and long distance running. He looked about as board as Jake was, keeping his eyes trained on the old forest road as he paced like a caged animal.

Leaning against a civilian-style black Hummer H2 was the spot commander for the Beta Watch team, Rachel Chance. Tan and tone, Rachel was the definition of sexy. Her black hair hung loosely to her mid-back. She had a figure to die for and was only eighteen years old. While Rachel wouldn't win a strength contest, everyone knew to watch out for this five-foot-three genius. She was an expert in hand-to-hand combat. Jake had heard that Rachel had a talent for strategic planning and that she helped with the setup of this mission.

One thing Jake questioned about RAW Troops was the order of their clothing. They were told that they would need to blend in to local populations and as such they would not be wearing fatigues. Jake wore only wind pants and a t-shirt. He was thankful for that, considering the heat. Blake wore a sleeveless flannel shirt underneath a pair of denim overalls, making him look like a farmer. Rachel on the other hand, wore jean shorts, a tank top, and knee high boots, all very high end and designer labels with a lot of expensive accessories and jewelry. Jake questioned Rachel's outfit, not knowing what women around here wore, but he was pretty certain that they didn't wear that expensive of clothing. More than one time during the day, Jake caught himself staring at her, and when Rachel realized it, she just smiled.

"Car." It was Rachel's soft voice that broke the silence for the first time in hours. Jake and Blake looked and saw an old pickup truck coming down the road. They quickly rushed into the woods, hiding, while Rachel continued to lean against the Hummer. The old pickup came to a stop and a tall man, with tight jeans and a flannel shirt got out. The man put on his Stetson hat as he got out and when he looked over Rachel he rubbed his chin and handlebar mustache.

"Damn big truck," the cowboy said, "for such a little girl. Need any help ma'am?"

"Name's Rachel," she said in her soft but confident, powerful voice. "Just waitin' for some friends to show up. Going hiking today."

"It's dangerous for a little lady to be at the edge of the woods alone," the cowboy said with a sly smile. "I'd better stay here and keep you safe until they come."

"Unnecessary," Rachel said with a smile. "I can take care of myself."

"How old are you?"

"Eighteen," Rachel said starting to get impatient. "And that's old enough to take care of myself."

"I'd better stay," the cowboy said as he took a step closer. "It's dangerous here. All kinds of rumors have been circulating around the area about military men and helicopters and what not. I haven't seen any of my friends from Whiterock for a few days now."

"What are you doing here then?" Rachel asked.

"Just passing through."

"Just passing through?"

"That's what I said," the cowboy said with a sneer.

"Then you best be on your way," Rachel said. "I don't need help."

"I think you do," the cowboy said.

The cowboy took a couple steps closer to Rachel and with his height and size; he had her cornered against the Hummer. Rachel smiled a soft smile, trying to hide how amused she was. The cowboy moved in closer and put his hand on Rachel's shoulder and put some force on it, making Rachel realize how strong he was. He moved in as if to kiss her, but as he got closer

Rachel pulled the Beretta pistol off the back of her belt and drove it underneath the guy's jaw. The guy stopped dead in his tracks, as his eyes grew wide. Rachel just smiled.

"Told you I could take care of myself," Rachel said with a laugh. "Why don't you get moving before my finger slips?"

"You wouldn't."

"You want to test that?"

The cowboy slowly backed away, got into his truck, and drove off. His tires spun as he tore out of the area. Rachel watched the truck until it was out of sight before opening the Hummer door and grabbing her EPD pistol. She clipped her Beretta back onto her belt as she looked around.

"Do you have any idea," Jake said as he and Blake walked out of the forest, "how dangerous that was? Pulling your gun on a civilian? Who in the hell do you think you are?"

"Quiet," Rachel said in a hushed voice as she scanned the area with her EDP pistol. "There's one nearby. I can feel it."

"Feel what?" Jake said harshly. "That cowboy's gonna call the police and we're all gonna be in trouble. Why didn't you signal us to come out of the trees?"

"There's one nearby," Rachel said, tension growing in her voice. "Look around for it."

"One what?" Jake said. "I'm sick of this. I'm sick of your lip. I'm sick of taking orders from a teenager." Jake pulled his gun on Rachel. "Damn it; tell us what's going on here."

There was tension all around, so thick you could cut it with a knife. Rachel was frozen, as was Blake, not knowing what to do. They both knew Jake had a temper at times, but he'd never acted like this before. Rachel knew what was wrong—a ghost was near them—but she couldn't tell them; she had her orders.

"I said," Jake barked, "tell me what's..."

Jake trailed off, as he turned as white as a ghost. He took two steps back allowing Rachel to see what he did. Jake was shaking like a leaf as urine started to travel down his leg. He reached for a gun that wasn't there as a ghost moved closer to him.

It was a middle-aged man, baldness starting to set in and slightly overweight. He wore a nice polo shirt and tan slacks with dress shoes. The man was dirty, and there were rips in his clothing. The group could see right through him. The man was merely an outline, barely recognizable as a human. He stumbled along with a trail of mist that seemed to follow his every move. When the ghost noticed the troops, he began to walk towards them.

"My son," the ghost wailed. "Please help me find my son."

Chapter #2

Gamma Ground Team

There hadn't been the slightest bit of movement anywhere. Kelly Grimes, spot commander for the Gamma Ground Team, felt a bit foolish hiding in a children's play fort, but the location was on the old forest road, and the fort was elevated high off the ground, making it the best position to watch the entrance and exit to Whiterock from. The fort was made of very basic wood strips, all scraps, nailed together on four pallets, mounted in a tree next to a swing set. The entrance ladder was composed of several boards nailed to the tree and the exit was either a slide or a fire pole. Kelly had laughed when she first entered the fort, thinking how much she would have loved to have a place like this as a kid.

Kelly tried to stand in the fort to stretch but the ceiling was too low for her six-foot, one-inch frame, especially since she was wearing brown cowboy boots. Kelly hated the outfit she was in, not that it looked bad, but the fact it was impractical for her mission today. The boots were new, not broken in, and were hurting her feet. Beyond that, they were hard to run in and she'd never worn boots like them before. She also wore boot cut blue jeans that were too tight in the waist and thighs topped off with a plain white tank top. She was supposed to have a red flannel shirt on over the tank top, but had taken that off within the first half hour due to the heat. Kelly worried that she would be at a great disadvantage since the jeans were so tight she couldn't maneuver quickly, even if she took the boots off.

Kelly ran her hand through her shoulder length blonde hair, feeling the dampness of it from her sweat. Just sitting in the fort was hard with the sweltering heat that was getting worse as the day progressed. Kelly had run out of water an hour ago. There was no breeze, but at least the sun wasn't beating directly down on her. Kelly sighed and spread herself out on the floor, twisting in an attempt to get her back to crack, which, after a short struggle, she was able to do. Kelly felt a little better and began to scan the area again.

She had a short range scoped out rifle that she used to scan the area. Being the oldest RAW member at the age of thirty-three, Kelly was one of the first RAW recruits, and was the best shooter at close and mid ranges. Having already served in other military divisions, Kelly was no stranger to covert action and hot zone fighting. Being one of the strongest of the women, and having led successful covert operations across the globe, Kelly was given the position as commander for the town of Whiterock and picked her own team comprised of women she had trained and trusted.

As she scanned the area, trying to think how long it had been since she'd seen movement, Kelly caught something moving out of the corner of her eye, Brady Hops. Brady, the youngest member of Kelly's team being only twenty-one years old, stood five-feet, six inches tall and had been a state champion in high school track, gymnastics, and swimming. Brady's body showed her athletics; she didn't have an ounce of fat on her. Brown hair in a messy braid, Brady jogged along the old forest road in white sneakers, running shorts, and a baggy black t-shirt that was tucked in front, but loose in the back concealing the two pistols she had clipped to the back of her shorts.

Kelly had given Brady the orders to stay out in the open, looking like she's going for a run, and circle the area. Kelly had seen Brady run by a number of times today, but she realized that

Brady was now heading to the fort with sweat pouring off of her. Kelly felt bad for not having enough water. She wouldn't be able to give any to Brady, even though she was feeling very parched herself.

As Kelly waited for Brady to make it to the fort, she looked over the pictures that were hung on the walls. It was all little children, no older than ten, who looked to be having the time of their lives. They were playing on the swing set and in the fort with parents who loved them very much. Kelly tried hard not to tear up thinking about the horrors that had happened to them, the pain and suffering and loss of life that had occurred because of a simple betrayal. Kelly brushed the tears away as Brady popped into the fort.

"We have an issue commander," Brady said as she kneeled in the fort.

"What?"

"I haven't seen anyone," Brady said, wringing the sweat from her shirt. "Erin and Maria included. I haven't seen anyone for a couple hours."

"Maybe they discovered something," Kelly said optimistically. "Maybe something came up."

"I followed S.O.P.," Brady said. "They didn't make it to the second check in, so I came back to the main base. I think we should look for them, I mean, what if they're in trouble?"

"Have you tried to communicate with them?"

"Once, about an hour ago. There was no reply."

"Try again."

Brady took out a cell phone she had clipped to the front of her shorts and flipped it open. She pushed a button on the side and the phone beeped. Brady waited, but there was no return beep—the signal from the others that all was well. Brady tried a couple more times with no luck, before she placed a call. They didn't answer. She hung up the phone and clipped it back to her belt, shaking her head.

Kelly was about to speak when they heard a strange sound outside the fort. It was one of the swings, swinging back and forth at a slow pace. The rusty chains were making a distinct noise. The pair stuck their head out the window of the fort and saw a small boy, no older than six, hair a mess, dirty clothes in tatters, having the most wonderful time on the swing, except for the fact that the girls could see right through him. He was a ghost, a spirit, not even aware that anything was wrong.

Kelly raised her rifle and sighted the boy in on her scope, but she hesitated, having a hard time pulling the trigger on someone so young. That's when it happened, the boy turned and looked directly at Kelly as he stopped swinging. Kelly froze in a panic while Brady reached her EPD pistol clipped to the back of her shorts. Brady wasted no time in sighting the boy in and pulling the trigger, causing the boy to disperse into a cloud of mist.

"What happened to no hesitation?" Brady asked as she put her pistol away.

"I'm sorry," Kelly said, trying to regain her composure. "That was just a little kid, like my brother when he was that age. Oh God, how did this happen? Who could have done this to these people?"

"Pull it together, Commander," Brady said as she slapped Kelly across the face. "These situations sucks, yes, but get it together. I thought you've been in combat before?"

"I have," Kelly said, rubbing her face where Brady had connected, "but not with children, not like this. We have a job to do so let's do it and get the hell out of here."

"Good," Brady said. "You got any water?"

"No," Kelly said holding up her canteen. "I've been out for some time now."

"I've been out too," Brady said. "We need to gather more supplies once we figure out what happened to Erin and Maria."

"What?"

"Erin and Maria," Brady said. "What should we do about them?"

Kelly thought it over for a moment. Erin Foltz was a computer genius and military royalty, having relation in every American war dating all the way back to the Revolution. Extremely shy, short, stocky, and level headed, Erin was the first person that Kelly had picked for her team. A late bloomer to the athletic side of combat, Erin could do anything with computers and electronics. Kelly's only hesitation about Erin was that she was shy and timid, but Kelly thought they could take care of her long enough to get her in the lab. Kelly knew Erin could open the high-tech electronics that guarded the lab.

Maria Diego was the conundrum of the group. She was of Brazilian and Moroccan heritage, born in the Caribbean, but raised in Russia. She had moved with her mother to the United States when she was sixteen after her father died. Kelly thought it was a little unnerving to see an island looking girl speak with a fluid Russian accent, but Maria was the real deal. Six feet tall, solid muscle and a black belt four times over. She was a world champion in three different martial arts and sword fighting. Maria didn't learn fighting for fun, where she grew up, she needed it for survival.

Kelly had faced Maria in different training and sparing sessions and quite honestly, was afraid of what she could do. Maria was a personable chatterbox, fluent in six different languages, but get on her bad side, and you'd see a temper that had no equal. Kelly knew, however, that Maria was one of the best sword fighters in the world and figured that if they were doing a house-to-house search, Maria with an EPD sword would be a great asset.

"We'd better go look for them," Kelly said. "We should stick together, though, at least until we find them."

"Good plan," Brady said. "Where do we start?"

"Where was the last place you saw them?"

"Near the school."

"Then that's where we start," Kelly said as she got up and grabbed her pack. "You ready?"

Brady nodded and the pair slipped out of the fort on the fire pole and started making their way towards the schoolhouse, a million thoughts running through Kelly's head as to what could have gone wrong.

Chapter #3

Delta Forest Team

A twig snapped underneath Mike Star's massive foot as he walked along the narrow trail in the woods. Mike, the spot commander for the Delta Forest Team, was in khaki cargo pants and a black t-shirt as he trudged along inside the forest. A nature lover by heart, Mike was content to be in the forest, hiking from one end to the other. A power lifter and endurance runner, Mike had won many triathlons and he knew there were very few people alive that could match him in strength or combat.

Hiking along with Mike were some of his best friends, Kevin Duff, Tim Rubin, and Gary Benson. The four men had been friends with each other since grade school. They had all joined the military together before moving on to the RAW troops. They constantly pushed each other to do better and they all wanted to be the best. They had all tried to get the spot commander position for the group. All the men looked the same: over six feet tall, extremely well-muscled, shaved heads, goatees, and the three others wore gym shorts and black t-shirts with hiking shoes.

It had been over an hour since they'd last shot a ghost. It was a competition for the men, to see who could the most. Mike was ahead, having shot four, but he knew it was still early in the day and they had a lot of ground to cover. Each man had a short range EPD rifle in their hand, along with an EPD pistol and Beretta pistol clipped onto their shorts. They were all unsure of the EPD design at first, but after the first few shots they realized the need for them.

Mike checked his GPS again, making sure they were on the right path. The Whiterock forest was filled with narrow trails, streams, and markers that only seemed to confuse non-locals. Mike realized without the GPS guiding them they would have been lost within the first half hour in the woods. They kept marching on, hoping to find something, when the trees finally broke, and they were at one of the main rivers.

"Hold up," Mike said with a commanding tone. "Let's take a breather."

The guys all took off their backpacks and got out some water and food. Both Tim and Gary took their shirts off and splashed water from the river onto their face and chests. Not only the heat, but also the July humidity was starting to get to the guys.

"How far to the farm, boss?" Tim asked.

"About another six miles," Mike said. "But this thick undergrowth is making this take longer than we estimated. We should make it to Blackstone Hollow with enough time to investigate before we enter the lab."

Kevin was about to speak when a shot rang out. It was in the distance and sounded like a massive rifle.

"Jade," Kevin said. "In the New Church spire. Are we going to swing past New Church and see how Jade and Dale are holding up? That's the third shot we've heard from her rifle."

"I'd rather swing into Whiterock," Tim said with a smile. "See how Maria is holding up. Did you see her this morning?"

"Jade looked much better," Kevin replied. "I couldn't take my eyes off her this morning. I've been working on her you know. We're going to be going out soon, maybe when this mission is over."

"Please," Gary said laughing. "You've been thinking that for the past year. Give it up man.

Rachel's much better looking though, and a lot more fun from what I've heard."

"They're identical twins," Mike said. "But how about we keep our minds on this mission. You know, ghosts, people getting their souls ripped from their bodies, that kind of stuff."

"We're just playing, boss," Tim said. "Trying to lighten the mood a bit."

"I know," Mike said. "I guess I'm just focused on all the ghost and goblin stories that I heard about these woods before we got here. They were haunted before the Whiterock Incident. There've been too many stories to discount."

"Don't tell me," Gary said, "that you believe in all that haunted garbage."

"How many ghosts have we seen today?" Mike asked. "How many have we shot?"

"That's different," Gary replied. "We know that sick doctor was messing with these people, doing stuff to them. They're the ghosts. I don't believe for one second that my dead parents could be floating around somewhere, haunting people. Stuff like that doesn't happen."

"If these ghosts can be real," Mike said. "Then the possibility exists that there could be other ghosts, made in different, possibly even natural, ways."

"That's hocus pocus, kid's nonsense," Tim said quickly. "There isn't any Ichabod Crane or Patrick Swayze types running around out here. That stuff doesn't exist."

"According to you," Mike said. "Look, there's something in these woods. We can all feel it. Evil. Doctor Tesla was never found. There have been no sightings or traces of him since he left New Church. No one knows what happened to him. What if he's still doing experiments out here?"

"Then we find him," Kevin said pulling the Beretta pistol off his shorts. "And we pull the trigger."

Mike was about to respond when an elk came out of the forest and walked up to the water, starting to drink. Kevin leveled his pistol at the elk and smiled.

"That'd be some good eating boss," Kevin said. "Stoke up a fire, a little fresh meat before we continue marching on."

"Holster that sidearm, solider," Mike ordered. "We don't have hunting permits."

"Hunting permits?" Kevin asked.

Before Mike could answer, Gary took his EPD rifle and shot the elk. It disappeared into a mist of air. The men stood silent for a moment.

"We have to watch for animals too?" Tim asked. "What else do we have to look out for in this stupid forest?"

"Pack it up, boys," Mike said. "We're moving out. If we go north, we'll eventually come to a bridge where we can cross the river. Let's go."

The men gathered their things and followed behind Mike. Mike wasn't sure how long it would take them to get to the bridge, but he had strict instructions that they were to cross the bridge, even though they could have very easily walked across the river at the point they were at.

The group trudged on. They made their way through the heavy undergrowth that lined the river. All the men kept a sharp eye out for anything out of the ordinary, not only the ghosts, but also any animals that might take their presence to be an intrusion of their territory. It took almost an hour, but they finally made it to the old wooden bridge. Mike was confused as to why they had to cross this bridge. It looked old and worn, ready to have fallen in the river over ten years ago. The group looked around the bridge and couldn't figure it out either.

"What's so special about this bridge boss?" Tim asked.

"Beats me," Mike said. "Search it. Anything you can find. We need to know what's going on here

"It's so odd," Gary said. "The trail leading to and from the bridge has long since been abandoned, yet they never moved or removed the bridge."

"Do we know who built it?" Kevin asked. "Or when?"

"No," Mike replied. "I was given strict orders to search it. There has to be something here that we need to find."

"Found it," Tim said, looking off to the side, past the trail. "There's a graveyard here. Right off the trail."

The men walked over and saw what Tim was looking at. Set in the trees, starting about fifty feet from the bridge, was a small cemetery. The rusted fence couldn't have been more than thirty feet by thirty feet, the gate rusted shut, and vines covering a majority of the monuments. The men slowly made their way inside and looked over the graves. They had to move branches, grass, and vines to see the names and dates that were carved into the stone. Most were so worn over that they were barely readable.

"Man alive, boss," Tim said, "the latest date I can make out is 1884. These are some old, old graves."

"I thought that New Church was the only burial site," Kevin said. "Everybody from Whiterock was supposed to be buried there. What's this place doing here?"

"These are Catholic graves," Gary said. "The verses are a dead giveaway. This is a Catholic cemetery whereas New Church was Episcopalian."

"Why so far out?" Tim asked. "And hidden in the forest?"

"When the Tassel family," Mike said, "started Whiterock and New Church they wanted everyone to attend New Church. There was no Catholic church and I'm assuming that many people here were Catholic. They needed their own place. But more to the point, why did we need to see this? Our guys must have known that this cemetery was here, why did they want us on the ground here? There must be something important here that we are supposed to see."

"What does Sepulchrum of Ornamentum mean?" Kevin asked.

"What?" Mike asked walking over to Kevin.

"Sepulchrum of Ornamentum," Kevin said. "This marker, it's the only thing written on it. No names, no dates, just Sepulchrum of Ornamentum."

"Hold the phone," Gary said pacing. "That's Latin for grave of ornaments...or equipment, loosely translated that is."

"What?" Mike asked.

"It means grave of equipment in Latin," Gary said. "Didn't anyone else pay attention in Latin class?"

"That was in eighth grade," Kevin said.

"It's what it means…I think," Gary said. "Do we dig? Find out what's there?"

As Mike was walking over the grave, he realized that the ground wasn't solid. He got down on his hands and knees and looked over the ground. Tim and Gary started looking too. It only took a moment to realize that they didn't need to dig, only move the cover that was on top. They moved the cover out of the way and saw a large metal casket inside, with a rope system ready to lift the casket out of the moist ground. Each man took a rope and began to pull. It only took a moment to get the modern style casket out of the ground. Mike opened the lid and the guys stood in awe of what they saw

Chapter #4

Zeta High Team

All was clear through Jade Chance's scope. Her position in the spire of New Church gave her a bird's eye view of the entire forest, the yard at the Tesla farm, and Whiterock itself. Jade continued to scan the yard, wondering if she should tell her spot commander that it had been over an hour since she'd last seen any movement, anywhere. No signs of the other teams; not even the Omega Entrance Team, stationed at the farm. Jade turned her gun towards Whiterock and continued to look but there was nobody there. Every person seemed to be hiding.

Dale Stein paced back and forth. He watched intently as Jade continued to look through her riflescope. He knew that Jade was the best long-range shooter in the RAW troops, but he thought the distance from the farm would be too much even for her, although she'd made shots of this distance in practice. The new EPD rifle Jade carried was the biggest gun Dale had ever seen, even bigger than the fifty caliber sniper rifles he'd used in his past military career and he'd been dying to see it in action.

Dale felt the weight of his smaller EPD shotgun in his hands. It felt too light to be an effective weapon, but they told him it was the only thing that would work on ghosts. Dale was glad to have it though. They met a ghost in the church right after the chopper had brought them there. They were walking into the church, through the graveyard, when they saw a man coming through the doors. They could see right through him. Dale quickly took the shot with his shotgun. Jade was stunned, but Dale was glad she saw one right away and knew what they were up against.

Dale was the spot commander here at New Church, but he wished he'd been with a different group, wished he could have been the spot commander for the Gamma Ground Team, since, Dale figured, being in the town would be where they would see the most action. Short, stocky, and strong as a bull, Dale was an amazing hand-to-hand combat fighter, absolutely deadly with any weapon at close range, and was one of the strongest in the Troopers. Dale had a chip on his shoulder. Five years ago, he had been the man to kill a dictator who was in hiding, but still ruling. Dale thought with that on his record, he should have been the one in charge of the whole operation. He'd put the operation together that killed the dictator, after all. But Jade's sister, Rachel, and another woman he didn't know, were the ones who put the show together. Dale was upset about it.

Dale was upset about his outfit today too. He wiped his brow, as he looked over the forest, drenched in sweat wearing a black formal suit, white long sleeved button up shirt, red tie, and black dress shoes. Being at the church, they thought he should be more formal. He thought Jade had the perfect outfit for today and her role.

Since Jade's rifle was going to be resting on the railing around the top of the spire, she knew she would be kneeling most of the day, so she would need to wear kneepads. Jade had black, gel-filled kneepads, black spandex volleyball shorts, a baggy blue t-shirt tucked into the shorts with the sleeves and sides cut out exposing her tone and tan core and her black sports bra underneath, along with black tube socks and red sneakers. Jade was fully dressed for a volleyball game, and in the intense heat of the day, the outfit was very comfortable, helping her stay in the kneeling position she'd been in for the past two hours.

Dale did think it odd that they chose the five-foot, three-inch woman to dress as a volleyball player. She seemed far too short to be taken seriously. Dale laughed to himself about how similar the eighteen-year old looked to her twin sister Rachel. The only way Dale could tell them apart was that Jade preferred her hair tied in a braid, whereas Rachel preferred hers loose.

Jade continued to look though her scope as Dale heard animals approaching from the south. Dale had thought it strange that they'd seen so few animals in this majestic forest, but he welcomed the chance to see some nature. If he couldn't be where the action was, he was determined to enjoy the view. He looked over the edge of the spire and saw two elk emerge from the forest and they started to eat some grass on the edge of the cemetery. Dale reached for his Beretta pistol. He wondered what Jade would think if he took the shot on one of the elk. As he thought about how tasty that elk would be, cooked over a slow fire, Dale noticed Jade's slender finger snaking its way onto the trigger of her gun. Dale grabbed his binoculars and looked towards the farm.

Jade's scope was trained in on a moose that had made its way into the farmyard. She wondered what would happen if an EPD shot would hit a living creature. Jade reached up and clicked up the magnification on her scope. The moose filled her viewfinder. Jade was about to continue scanning the yard when the moose turned and looked directly at her. Jade could feel the beast's stare upon her. She wasted no time in squeezing the trigger. The blast from the massive gun was deafening and it pushed Jade slightly back as the moose dispersed into a cloud of mist.

"Nice shot," Dale said still looking in the binoculars. "You hit it right in the head."

"That's what I was aiming for," Jade said as she scanned the yard through her scope. "I didn't know that we were going to have to deal with ghost animals too. What else is out here?"

"I don't know," Dale said softly. "We just have to keep our eyes and ears open."

"I wish I knew how my sister was doing," Jade said, turning towards Dale. "We haven't had any reports yet? Haven't heard any word from anyone have we?"

"There's been no communications," Dale said. "Not from anyone. I'm sure everyone is busy. Have you seen anything in Whiterock?"

Jade pivoted the gun. She scanned the town, but didn't see any movement. The only thing she'd ever seen in the town was Brady Hops, jogging down one of the streets. At one point, she thought she saw someone, hiding in a fort next to a swing set near the main road, but she couldn't get any confirmation on a person or ghost there. Jade continued to scan all over the town, around the churches, school, and city hall. There was no sign of anybody. This made Jade nervous as she felt she should have been able to find at least one member of Gamma Ground Team.

"I don't see anything," Jade said looking at Dale. "It's quiet as a tomb down there. Wait, hang on, that's a bad metaphor right now. I mean there's no one moving down there, I can't see anything. I don't mean that everyone's dead, like in a tomb. There's nothing there, I mean..."

"I get it," Dale said interrupting. "You nervous?"

"Why?" Jade asked surprised. "Do I seem nervous? Have my actions been nervous or not up to what you expect? Is there something wrong with my performance or abilities today?"

"No," Dale said with a laugh. "You're just rambling. It seems like you're nervous about something. Granted, there's a lot to be nervous about, it just seems like it's affecting you."

"I always ramble," Jade said. "I guess that's how I just talk. Always has been that way. I may be a little nervous, this being my first mission and all. I was really hoping that my sister would have been the spot commander for me. Nothing against you, you're doing a fine job and all, but I wanted to be with her."

"I get it," Dale said. "Just stay focused. Keep your eyes on the farm; you're doing a great job, Jade."

Jade turned her gun back to the farm. Scanning the yard, she worried about her sister. There was still no movement inside the farmyard, and the silence of the forest was beginning to upset her. There were no sounds of animals or birds. There was a ghostly quiet within a forest that should be an orchestra of sound. Through her scope, Jade noticed movement inside the farmyard. She scanned the yard, but couldn't see what had caught her eye. Jade moved away from the scope and looked at the farm through her binoculars. There was still nothing there. Jade put her eye back in the scope and felt her blood run cold. A man was staring back at her. A man that was transparent and hovering off the ground. Jade felt a chill run down her spine. Even in the intense heat of the day, she felt cold. Jade fire her gun as quickly as she could. The man dispersed in a cloud of mist as Jade stood up quickly and paced around before taking a drink from her canteen.

"Everything okay?" Dale asked.

"No," Jade said harshly. "I felt something when he looked at me. I can't explain it. Maybe that's the feeling of pure evil or something. It was like a dark, cold, wet blanket was being draped over me, and I couldn't escape it. That was a horrible feeling, Dale. I don't know how else to describe it."

"Shake it off, solider," Dale said. "Keep your wits about you. We have a long way to go yet out here."

"But I feel so strange," Jade said as she went back to her scope. "I don't know. My emotions are running wild and I can't control them. One second I want to cry, the next I want to kill something, the next I just want to be held. It's not like anything I've ever gone through before."

"Hang on," Dale said raising his gun. "They said these things would affect you when they're near. There must be some inside the church or on the grounds close by. That's what's causing your problem."

Jade was about to respond when they heard footsteps coming up the stairs. They both froze and waited. After a moment a man appeared. Not much of a man, short, hunched over, what was left of his gray, stringy hair was a mess while his brown suit barely clung to his slender frame. He coughed as he looked at Dale with sad eyes, the pungent aroma of body odor and death filling the air, as he got closer.

Dale kept his gun leveled off, finger on the trigger, waiting for any sign that this man was human or ghost. In an instant, a puff of mist filled the air, coming from this man's shoulders. Dale took a breath and froze, as the man got closer, a menacing grin appearing on his face as he locked eyes with Dale. Dale wanted to pull the trigger but something prevented him as he heard a gunshot go off. Dale spun around to see Jade, holding her

EPD pistol. The man had dispersed into a cloud of mist and instantly gone away.

"Nice shot kid," Dale said with a smile. "You don't hesitate. I like that."

"Someone had to shoot him," Jade said. "I get the feeling that there are more of them here. I can still feel that something, or someone, is here with us."

Just then, more footsteps were heard coming up the stairs. This time, a little girl, no more than ten years old, stepped into the spire. Her red hair was dirty and filled with leaves, her skin was covered in a layer of dust, her yellow romper was tattered and dirty, and she was crying. Massive alligator tears were rolling down her cheeks as she looked at Jade and Dale. Jade swallowed hard and aimed her gun. She could see directly through the little girl. It took everything Jade had, but she pulled the trigger and the girl dispersed into a cloud of mist.

"Okay," Jade said putting her pistol back in its holster. "I don't want to do that again. That was just a little kid. I mean, she was so little, how can anything be this evil as to destroy the lives of people like this?"

Tears started to roll down Jade's face as she turned away from Dale. She didn't want him to see her like this. Jade felt horrible for what she just had to do, and she knew that if another little kid came into her view she would have to do it again. The weight of what had happened to this place started to come down on Jade and she cried harder. She wanted to run. She wanted to run away and leave this behind, and that made her cry even worse because she knew that these weren't her true feelings.

"What's the problem?" Dale asked, putting his large hand on Jade's shoulder. "This is war. These kinds of things happen. Having to shoot people you don't want to; not the ghost thing."

"Can I make a confession?" Jade asked.

"Of course."

"The only reason I'm here," Jade said between sobs, "is because of Rachel. She wanted to be involved with RAW Troops and I followed her. We do everything together. I'm not cut out for this kind of action."

"You're doing fine," Dale said not knowing exactly how to handle this. "Just hang in there, Jade. This will be over soon."

"Damn it," Jade said wiping the tears away and composing herself. "I wanted this. Damn it all to hell. Why am I like this today? I've never been like this before. Normally I'm the strong one between us. Emotionally, I mean. This is so out of character for me. There must be more of those things hanging around. Would you do a quick search of the church building and see what you can find? See if there are any more of those things around?"

"Of course," Dale said. "Keep watching the farm and shout if you need anything."

"Thank you," Jade said as she looked into the scope.

Chapter #5

Theta Water Team

Two canoes cut silently through the water. They'd only entered the forest five minutes ago, but its beauty already impressed them. Larissa Abercrombie kept a sharp eye on the water's edge on both sides, not wanting to be surprised by anything or anyone. She knew of all the animals that live in the forest, and she knew all the dangers now native to the area. She'd been the first one to read Ethan's journal as the extraction chopper was leaving New Church. Larissa had been with the team sent to retrieve the journal when a communication came that Ethan, Michelle, and Madison were at New Church, needing an airlift extraction...a communication that now seemed contradictory to other information that they had.

Larissa, the spot commander for the Theta Water Team, was a twenty-eight year old water expert. A champion swimmer and water-skier, Larissa was the only choice to lead the team exploring the waters. A petite, five-foot blonde, wearing only a one-piece lifeguard swimsuit and aqua socks, Larissa still wondered who sent the message that the trio needed help and why they weren't in the church when the chopper arrived. Larissa had been chosen for the leader of the extraction team due to her performance in training. Larissa was a genius that could think and adapt faster than anyone else in the RAW Troops.

Larissa was unsure about the rest of her team, though. In the canoe with her was Kayla Johnson, a tall, twig-like twenty-year old South African girl. Kayla was a newer member of the RAW Troops. Wearing a black bikini, full coverage halter-top and boy shorts bottoms, Kayla didn't seem to stand out athletically or strategically, but she came recommended by the tactical commander.

The other canoe held Bradley Fischer and Trey Hicks, both big, well-muscled men wearing black swimming trunks. Bradley was the only man in RAW with long hair as his shoulder length brown hair hung loosely around his big head. Trey was shaved bald. Larissa had trained with both of the men and, while they looked impressive, she felt that they didn't push themselves to their full potential and she knew that Trey didn't like her to begin with; she'd shown him up in training and rejected his romantic offers.

Larissa kept her eyes peeled. She had an EPD pistol clipped to the back of her suit, along with a Beretta and an EPD rifle near her feet. Kayla had the same weapons, and the guys had identical pistols, but they carried EPD shotguns instead of rifles. Larissa had also made sure that they carried both regular and EPD knives. They'd yet to have to use any of the weapons, but Larissa did tell the group what was in the forest. They hadn't seemed to believe her, but they were aware that strange things were going on.

Larissa knew that her team had the most complex mission. They had to navigate the waters of the forest, checking out different sites, including the old mill. When they had finished, they needed to get to Blackstone Hollow to meet with Delta Forest Team to enter the lab. The biggest problem Larissa knew they would encounter was the complicated waterway system; they could easily get lost. Larissa had wanted to kick Trey off the team when they arrived. He had made a sexist joke about Larissa using the GPS to guide them through the forest.

The group paddled on, entering the forest from a northern point on the main river. Larissa had ordered the group to travel in silence. This was not only for everyone's protection, but she heard Trey and Bradley talking on the way out and she was not impressed with either of the men. They gossiped like children and she didn't want to have to listen to them all day.

After a half hour in the canoes, they entered the first area they needed to inspect: the swimming hole. They shored the canoes and began exploring the area. It was exactly like Ethan had described it in his journal, even down to the volleyball net in the shallow part of the water. Larissa walked around the outer edge, right against the forest. Bradley and Trey stayed in the water, walking in the pond, while Kayla stayed on the opposite edge. They all had their EPD pistols at the ready as they walked around. After about five minutes, the group hadn't found anything that seemed strange or out of place.

"This site is a bust, Larissa," Kayla said walking up to her. "There's nothing here. Why did we have to stop?"

"The journal mentioned this place many times," Larissa said as she waved Bradley and Trey in. "We had to make sure that there was nothing here. We have a lot of spots like this to visit, so get used to it."

"This whole mission is a bust," Trey said. "It's all a scam, Larissa. I mean ghosts? Are you serious?"

"Trey," Larissa said stepping right into his face. "Follow orders. A lot of people, good people, have died in this area and I'm not going to be one of them because you don't take your job seriously."

"Just saying, girl," Trey said. "It's a wild goose chase."

"Do not call me, 'girl,'" Larissa said raising her voice. "Don't ever call me that again."

"Okay, woman," Trey said laughing.

Larissa wasted no time in punching Trey. Trey wasn't expecting a fist, nor was he ready for it. Trey took a step back as Larissa rushed him. Larissa tried to take Trey to the ground but he was far too powerful for her. Trey lifted Larissa up in a fluid motion, twisting, so she would land on her back with him on top; exactly as Larissa had anticipated that he would do. In the split second that Larissa was in the air, she grabbed her pistol that was clipped to the back of her suit and as she landed and Trey positioned himself on top of her, Larissa jammed the gun into Trey's lower jaw.

"First rule of fighting big man," Larissa said looking up at Trey as fear washed over him and he froze, "I could have shot you before you had me on the ground; never, and I mean never, let your guard down. Don't push me again. Follow the damn orders or you will be considered in subordinate and mutinous. Do I make myself clear?"

"Yes," Trey said. "Now put that thing away before you hurt someone."

Larissa held the gun on his jaw for a moment longer before she pulled it back and Trey got off of her. Both stood up as Larissa paced around the area, looking at the exit stream then back to the canoes.

"Let's go," Larissa said walking back to the canoes. "We need to keep moving."

As the group got back into the canoes, Trey kept his eyes fixed on Larissa. She realized that what she did was very stupid. He posed no threat to her; in the command process that is, but since she humiliated him in front of the group he would be looking for revenge. Anything and everything she did would be criticized and questioned by him. Larissa knew that before the day was out she would probably have to fight him again, a fight she would lose if she didn't jump him by surprise again. Her only hope was that they would see a ghost soon and he would be scared to death, forgetting about what had happened at the swimming hole.

Chapter #6

Jake and Blake were frozen in terror, unable to even move. Rachel quickly sighted the man in her EDP pistol and pulled the trigger. When the EPD charge hit the ghost an explosion of mist filled the air and the ghost was gone. Everyone just looked blankly at where the ghost had been, the mist hanging in the air. It took a moment before anyone could talk again.

"What the hell was that?" Jake's voice trembled.

"That was a spirit," Rachel said putting her pistol away. "The slowest and dumbest class of ghost we will be dealing with today."

"Wait, ghost?" Blake asked. "You cannot be serious."

"What did we just see?" Rachel asked. "Just before we saw him, Jake disobeyed orders, broke protocol, and tried to kill me. Why?"

"I don't know," Jake said still trembling. "I don't know what came over me. It was like I couldn't control it. I'm so sorry, Rachel."

"Don't be," Rachel said as she playfully punched him in the arm. "I didn't behave as I normally would have either. I was told that these things affect you when they are nearby. Your behavior will change and you will feel weird when they're near. If you start to get emotional, you can be sure that one is nearby."

"But how?" Jake asked. "And what did you mean by classes we'd see today?"

"Victor Tesla," Rachel said as she leaned against the truck again, "was working on a weapon—a warrior—something that couldn't be killed. This is what he came up with. The entire town of Whiterock was turned into ghosts. Dr. Tesla's lab is hidden underneath this forest and we don't know what's down there. That's why we're here."

"What do they want?" Blake asked.

"The spirit we saw," Rachel continued, "doesn't know he's dead. Basically mindless and slow; some are aggressive, some aren't. You could think of them as an inverted zombie, a soul without a body. I know there are four classes of them, but I was only informed about two of them: spirits and shadows. We just saw a spirit, dumb and slow, doesn't know it's a ghost, and still thinks it's alive. A shadow knows that it's dead and will try to kill you."

"If you're killed by one of those things," Blake asked, his voice trembling, "do you become one?"

"That depends," Rachel said. "If the one we just met did, no, although, he would have no reason to kill. A shadow wouldn't turn you either, but I've heard the higher classes are super aggressive and can strip the soul right from the body."

"Do we have to worry about zombies running around?" asked Jake. "A body without a soul."

"No," Rachel said laughing. "If a higher class strips the soul out, it uses that soul to gain strength, become more powerful."

"So, what is our full mission?" Jake asked. "And why didn't you tell us about this before?"

"I didn't tell you," Rachel said, "because those were the orders. I don't know, maybe they thought you wouldn't believe them or something. Our first mission is containment. Make sure the ghosts don't leave the forest. Each RAW unit is at a point where ghosts were sighted. We are waiting for Alpha Strike Force to get here. They will be flying in by chopper, at which point we are to head to the Tesla farm to meet up with the other teams and enter the lab. We are trying to locate Dr. Tesla and a number of other people that were mentioned in our field report. We are also trying to figure out what city Dr. Tesla might unleash these ghosts on next. For now, we destroy any ghosts that we see and wait for the chopper. Jake, take some water and get yourself cleaned up."

Rachel opened the Hummer and grabbed a water bottle, handing it to Jake before she grabbed some EPD rounds and reloaded her gun. Jake went behind the Hummer and washed his legs off before getting some new pants and drawers from his bag. Jake wasn't embarrassed as he figured that anyone who saw a ghost for the first time would also wet themselves.

The trio passed the next couple of hours in fear. They watched the road and waited. Two other cars came by in that time. One was a group of college girls that were making a photo journal of the state for a college class. They wanted to go to Whiterock to take pictures, but Rachel wouldn't let them. She showed them her military ID, but they didn't believe her, not in the outfit she was wearing. It was then that Rachel questioned the setup of the RAW troops. If she'd been wearing military fatigues, she'd have had no problem handling these girls. Rachel had to flash a signal to Blake and Jake, who came out of the woods with guns that led the girls to leave. The other vehicle was another old pickup truck that didn't even slow as it passed by.

As the sun began to set, two cars came into sight. Like always, Jake and Blake disappeared into the woods, while Rachel leaned up against the Hummer. She watched as two state police cars pulled up and four cops got out, their guns drawn on Rachel.

"Hands in the air," one of the cops shouted as the four moved in on Rachel. "No sudden movements or we will shoot. Hands above you head and turn around."

Rachel frowned. She realized that the cowboy she pulled the gun on must have called the police. She also realized that when she turned around they would see the Beretta clipped to the back of her belt. Rachel followed the orders and put her hands behind her head and turned around. In the reflection of the window of the Hummer Rachel saw one of the cops put his gun away and pull out his handcuffs. The cop slammed Rachel against the Hummer, pulled the gun off of her, and cuffed her hands behind her back.

"I have a permit for that, guys," Rachel said hoping to get out of this. "I'm military."

"Bull," barked the cop who was cuffing her. "We got a call you pulled that and were shooting at someone trying to help you."

"Trying to rape me was more like it," Rachel said.

"Shut it, ma'am," the cop said. "Where's your identification?"

"Back pocket."

The cop pulled out Rachel's wallet and looked at the military badge that she had inside. He scoffed at it as he handed it to the other cops. They made hushed comments that Rachel couldn't hear, but she could hear laughing.

"No way," the cop said returning to Rachel. "No way are you military or that you are eighteen. I would guess fifteen at best."

"Blake, Jake! Come on out," Rachel called. "I should warn you I have two other soldiers with me. They are posted in the woods and they will not take kindly to me being treated this way."

The police aimed their guns into the woods, but no one came out. They kept watching, as did Rachel, but no one was there. Rachel didn't understand it. She knew she felt a little off, and was pretty sure that there was a spirit around, but she didn't know where.

"Nice try, kid," the cop said laughing as he slammed Rachel against the Hummer again. "Any other weapons?"

Rachel said nothing as the cop started patting her down. He ran his hands along her silky smooth legs, over her shorts, under her tank top around her stomach, and when he felt Rachel's chest, she'd had enough. Rachel used her heel to kick the cop in the shin and when he took a step back, she kicked up, connecting with his groin. The cop bent over in pain and he bent low enough for Rachel to grab the guy's neck. Even though she was in cuffs, she got him in a nerve hold and the cop passed out.

"Think a civilian could do that?" Rachel asked the other cops, as they stood there dumbfounded. "Now quick looking dumb and take these cuffs off me."

The cops didn't move or say anything. They were too busy looking at the edge of the forest. Rachel looked to where they did and she had to swallow in a dry throat. She saw Blake, Jake, and a large man walking towards them; they were all ghosts. The cops were freaking out, not knowing what to do. The cops open fired, but their bullets had no effect on the shadows. Rachel quickly stepped through the cuffs so her arms were in front of her and opened the Hummer. She grabbed her EPD pistol. Rachel wasted no time in shooting every one of the ghosts, but it was too late. They'd already killed the cops.

Rachel franticly searched through the cop that had cuffed her but she couldn't find the cuff keys before all the cops had switched. Rachel dispatched the cop ghosts and reloaded her gun, thankful that all the cops had been spirits so they died with one shot, before she returned to look for the keys. Rachel found the keys and removed the cuffs as she assessed the situation. She looked over the mess that had just happened and held back a tear.

She was alone. She couldn't remember a time when she'd been this scared. Uncertain of what to do, but knowing she had to act quickly; Rachel reasoned that she needed to get together with another group in the area. They were given strict instructions not to be alone and that ghosts would congregate in a spot. Her twin sister, Jade, was stationed at New Church with a sniper rifle. Rachel believed that she'd heard the rifle go off a couple times during the day, but she wasn't sure. She also knew that walking through the forest alone would be a problem. Rachel decided to meet up with the group that was stationed inside Whiterock.

She quickly hefted all the bodies into the two police cars and took all the weapons and ammunition from them. If her plan didn't work, she didn't want some kids stumbling upon the arsenal there. Once she had all the weapons cleared out, Rachel went into the woods to look for her teammates. She found them lying in a ravine, looking so peaceful, so happy. Rachel didn't really care for either Jake or Blake, but they were teammates, and that had to count for something. Rachel grabbed their weapons and headed back to the Hummer.

Rachel organized everything she needed and loaded up the Hummer before grabbing a cloth from the truck and ripping it in two. She stuffed the strips into the gas tanks of the police cars and then lit them on fire before dashing to the Hummer and quickly driving a safe distance away. She only had to wait a moment before both cars, and the bodies inside, were engulfed in an inferno. She watched for a moment before taking off and heading for Whiterock.

Chapter #7

Erin sat trembling in a closet, sobbing at the predicament that she'd gotten Maria and herself into. Maria was standing, anxious and tense, like a caged animal waiting to break out and attack. Erin could feel the adrenaline rushing through Maria and wished they could get out of the closet. Erin knew it was her fault they were in there. She understood that it was her fault they'd lost their packs containing their water, food, phones, and maps. Maria had already scolded her enough over it and she knew that Kelly would discipline her as well.

It had started simple enough. Erin and Maria were going to investigate the school. Maria led the way, her EPD sword drawn, and Erin followed with her EPD gun at the ready. On a normal day, Maria would tower over Erin, but today, Maria's outfit required her to wear black boots, with six-inch heels and two-inch platforms, making her look like a giant. The boots went up to her knees. The boots matched Maria's sparkling, blood red, halter dress, clinging to her skin all the way to the hem, with a slit up the left side. It was a fancy, formal dress and Maria accessorized it well. Maria looked more ready for a party than a bloodbath with ghosts.

Erin, in her hiking boots, short khaki shorts, and plain white tank top, had wanted to look over the school, even though Maria was against it. Going through houses was one thing, but the school was a much bigger building, but Erin had a feeling about it. They crept through the school and Maria had to battle with a number of ghosts. Every time, Maria would disperse them with her sword, Erin had yet to fire a shot today. As they got deeper into the school, Erin found what she wanted to see.

They entered the main office and Erin booted up the computers. Erin took her Yankees baseball cap off and let her shoulder length brown hair down. When the computer was up and running, Erin started hacking. She was trying to discover any information that she could on what happened and she figured that, even though school was on summer break when the Whiterock Incident happened, there might be something about it on the computers. As Erin worked, Maria noticed that ghosts were gathering outside the door.

Erin was working on getting the principal's emails when the ghosts started coming though. Maria pulled her from the chair and they rushed through the building, not bothering to grab their bags. They rushed through doors, fighting off what ghosts they could, when they were cornered and forced to enter a classroom. Inside, they entered another door, but it was a closet. They both had prepared for the worst, but the ghosts never entered the closet. They'd been in there for over an hour and neither dared to look out into the room.

"We're going to die in here right?" Erin asked, breaking the silence. "And we're going to end up like those monsters out there."

"Don't assume that," Maria said with her heavy Russian accent. "We didn't check in twice. Standard operating procedure says they should team up and start looking for us. They knew we were going to the school. Kelly and Brady should be here soon Erin. Don't worry and stop crying."

"What if they don't?" Erin asked through her tears. "What if they've been taken too? How long can we stay here?"

"You don't stop crying," Maria said with a vengeful tone. "You won't need to worry about those things out there. Now quiet, there's a way out of every trap. We just need to think of it."

In the dim light, both girls looked over the large coat closet. Maria's first thought had been to go through the ceiling, but it was solid, unlike the suspended ceiling in the rest of the building. The floors and walls were solid as well, and there wasn't anything that could be used to cut with. In searching the coats and jackets, Maria had found a cell phone with a dead battery—useless. Maria's mind raced, but she was getting no ideas when the knob on the door started to turn.

Erin and Maria both braced themselves for the worst, but breathed a huge sigh of relief when the door opened and two teenagers were standing there. It was a boy and a girl, possibly twins, both looked around seventeen, blonde hair, blue eyes, fair skin, tall and solidly built, the boy wearing only jeans and sneakers, the girl jeans, tank top, and sneakers. They were dirty and tired. Their skin glistened with sweat as they stared confusedly at Erin and Maria. Maria gathered her wits and brought her sword right into the boy's face. The boy didn't even flinch as a sly smile grew on his face. Erin realized that the girl was holding onto their packs.

"You have our packs," Erin said meekly. "Can we have them back?"

"What are you doing here?" the girl asked. "Who are you?"

"We're with the military," Maria said, barking with power behind her voice. "Give us our packs back right now."

"You don't look military to me," the boy said with a sneer.

"Maybe they can help us, Brandon," the girl said. "This is my brother, Brandon. I'm Lisa."

"Twins?" Erin asked.

"Yes," Lisa said. "We saw you enter the school and saw you get cornered in here. We waited for those things to leave."

"Those things use to be our friends and family," Brandon said, "...until the military moved in and changed them."

"We want to prevent that," Erin said, "from ever happening again."

"Then call your friends," Lisa said tossing Erin the pack. "I'm sure there are more of you. Call them and tell them to come here. We have some startling news about these things. Something Brandon and I discovered."

Erin started digging in the pack for her phone, but Maria kept the sword on Brandon. Brandon kept his ground and was in a stare down with Maria. In an instant Maria drove her sword into Brandon's chest and he stumbled backwards, mist coming off his body. Maria swung at him twice more with blinding speed and on the second hit, Brandon dispersed into mist. Maria pointed the sword at Lisa, who was in a defensive position, but she was laughing.

"We discovered," Lisa said with a chuckle, "what we are. We know. We know everything: how we were separated, how long we have, and what we can do. Being separated causes a strange reaction. Death begets death and all we want to do is kill."

"You can talk," Maria said sarcastically. "We thought all you things were for the most part brainless."

"You're the brainless ones," Lisa said.

"I saw right through you two," Maria countered. "The instant you opened the door I knew that you were ghosts. You tried to set a trap for us. Let us cower in here for a bit, pretend to save us so we call our friends here then you get to satisfy your bloodlust."

"You're somewhat smart," Lisa said mockingly. "For someone who's alive."

Before Lisa could continue, Erin open fired with her EPD pistol, unloading all fifteen rounds into Lisa point blank. Lisa just laughed and threw Erin across the room. Erin hit the wall on the other side about four feet above the ground, cracking the sheetrock before falling to the ground in a pile. Maria gasped at the power of this ghost. Lisa moved towards Maria, who lifted her sword up and tried to swing but Lisa was able to dodge every attempted strike.

Lisa pushed Maria back, slamming her into a wall. She tried to rush Maria, but Maria was able to keep the ghost at bay with her sword. Erin was trying to stand, but was still dazed from the throw. Lisa finally got inside Maria's guard and pushed her up against the wall, lifting her feet off the ground, and holding her in the air.

"Be afraid girl," Lisa said with a menacing tone. "Be very afraid."

Maria swore at Lisa in Russian, calling her all sorts of horrible names. Lisa just smiled at her, getting ready to rip the soul right from her body, until she felt an EDP knife drive into her skull. Erin had gotten up and had grabbed one of the knives that Maria kept in the bag. Erin took a couple steps back while Maria used her sword to take multiple swings at Lisa, finally cutting her down with a swipe across the throat, causing Lisa to disperse into mist. Maria wordlessly rushed from the closet, motioning Erin to follow. Erin grabbed the packs as Maria picked up a chair and threw it through a window as ghosts started to pour into the room. The girls wasted no time in using the new exit.

Chapter #8

"These are EPD guns," Kevin said looking over the contents. "Who the hell would have buried them out here? Why?"

"Ghost Town Labs," Mike said. "Their symbol is imprinted into every one of these guns. Look at this."

Mike pulled a small book from the casket. He looked over the three pages that were inside of it.

"This is from Doctor Victor Tesla himself," Mike said. "Instructions on how to use these guns and their design. He says they are for destroying the ghosts. They were made about three years ago and it says here that these weapons, electricity, and fire are the only known ways to disperse the ghosts. They wanted to have some arms in the vicinity in case of an incident."

"They got their incident," Kevin said with a sneer. "We take these guns?"

"Yes," Mike said. "Everybody, carry as many as you can while still being able to travel. Get all the ammo you can, we need to move out."

The men loaded up the weapons in their backpacks before putting the casket back in the ground, returning the cover so the grounds wouldn't look disturbed. They carefully crossed the bridge and made their way back into the forest. Mike wasn't sure if he was supposed to do more in the cemetery or not, but he felt there was no point in wasting time. He had more missions to take care of in the woods and they were already behind schedule.

The deeper into the forest the men got, the slower going it was. The undergrowth had never been taken care of and the old growth of the forest had many downed trees, brush, and bushes that slowed the trek. Mike thought that one good match during a dry season would have really helped the place, and he was amazed there'd never been a forest fire to clean the floor of the forest off. Although they'd heard a couple of rifle blasts in the distance, from Jade at New Church for sure, they'd had no other signs of their other groups. Mike wondered when the next stop would come, being exhausted from the heavy walking, when the forest gave way to a small meadow, complete with a pond.

"Take five, men," Mike said, sitting down next to the water, taking out his canteen and a piece of beef jerky. "We need to rest for a minute."

"Do we have the time?" Gary asked. "I mean, we're moving slower than we expected. Are we going to make it to Blackstone Hollow in time?"

"Don't worry," Mike said. "We'll get there in good time. No point in pushing on if we fall over in the woods."

"This heat is killing all of us," Tim said. "I can barely stand it."

"It's like Doctor Tesla," Kevin said, "has opened the gates of hell. Or at least brought its temperatures here."

"Look at that," Gary said pointing. "Is that what I think it is?"

Everyone looked to where Gary was pointing and they saw a fort built into the woods, on the edge of the meadow. It was slightly hidden and hard to spot, but it was there. The men walked up to it and looked it over. Using four trees as main posts, someone had created a ten-foot by ten-foot fort, about six feet off the ground. Old logs made up the walls, with a mud plaster seal, and a multi-layered branch roof covered it. The door was simply a trap in one of the corners. Mike lifted the trap cover off and stuck his head in. He used his arms to pull himself in, followed by Tim. They motioned that no one else could enter, the fort itself being too small.

Inside the fort was very basic. A small mattress with a sleeping bag and a storage shelf with candles, empty beer cans, booze bottles, sports magazines, and an empty box of condoms. Hanging from the ceiling was a bag full of empty food cans. The smell of the food cans, along with very stale body odor, was the only thing they could smell inside the fort.

"Someone was living here," Tim said, looking over the bag. "Must have been here for quite a while."

"The incident happened three days ago," Mike said. "Possibly someone could have escaped the city and fled out here. But where are they now? Are they still human or have they been turned?"

"If they were still human," Tim said. "I would bet you a steak dinner that when they heard the rifle blasts from New Church, they ran there. It would be the logical thing to do."

"How so?" Mike asked.

"If you've been alone for a couple days," Tim said. "Without any human contact, thinking that everyone is dead, and you heard what could only be described as a military rifle being shot, after they were air lifted in with a chopper, wouldn't you seek them out?"

"It's possible," Mike said. "But just as likely that whomever was here is now dead, or a ghost. Either way, we need to keep moving."

Mike made his way out of the fort and back into the meadow. Tim followed, after circling around the fort looking for any clues as to the whereabouts of the final inhabitant. There was nothing of note. The total lack of evidence was a clue in itself, the person here wanted to leave no trace so they went out of their way to cover their tracks.

The men took a final drink from their canteens and headed back into the forest. Mike didn't want to tell them that they were further behind than he'd led on. He knew that everyone was tired, and tempers were wearing thin in the heat of the day. Mike knew they had to push on, get to Blackstone Hollow before the chopper flew over the forest. He was desperate to see Blackstone Hollow, see a city hidden so deep from everything, and he knew that there would be a lot of trouble when they got there.

After another hour of hiking through the forest, the sun was setting on the horizon, an explosion had been heard somewhere in the forest, and more shots had rang out from New Church, when the men finally broke through the forest and set eyes on Blackstone Hollow. The men walked around the stone fence that surrounded the city. Mike hadn't told them what they were going to see, he didn't really know himself. They were simply told of decaying ruins hidden in the forest, but nothing like what they were seeing here.

"What is this place?" Kevin asked.

"Legend says that the family of Jacob Meeks built it with government help. Never had many people living in it," Mike said.

"Incredible," Tim said looking over the gallery between the city hall and the church. "The history of this place. If only these buildings could talk. What would they say? What would the story of this place be? Who in their right mind would want to live in a place like this? What would the buildings say if they could talk?"

"They'd say burn us to the ground," Kevin said. "This place is a death trap. Who knows what kind of wild animals are living in these buildings. We should move along before we become supper."

"Speaking of supper," Tim said looking at his watch. "It is about that time boss. What say we snipe out a deer or something? I'm betting we have to search every one of these buildings. We could cook it on a fire while we search."

"Damn it, Tim," Mike said frustrated. "What did I say before? We don't have permits and we're on a mission here. You've got all the food you need in your pack. Now, you're right, we have orders to search every building here."

"Why?" Kevin asked. "What could possibly be worth our time in this place?"

"Are you kidding?" Mike said. "Look around us. This place is ground zero for a Ghost Town Incident. This town is hidden in the woods and the government has no intelligence on it. They knew about the graveyard at the bridge; they must have known about the guns. We must find something to stop the madness that's been going on in this place. We must prevent it from ever happening again. We have to search everything."

"Split up?" Gary asked.

"In pairs," Mike said. "Tim, you come with me and we go to the southwest. Gary and Kevin, you two go to the northeast corner and work your way towards us."

"You got it boss," Gary said as he led the way to the north.

Mike and Tim walked to the southwestern corner of the city. A rather large foundation with post corners still standing and a partial wall. Tim placed his hand on the wall and it crumbled, taking most of the wall with it. The floor was still solid enough to stand on, and Mike led the way to a stairwell. Both men took their pistols out of their holsters and aimed them towards the ground as they started their way down the creaking stairs.

At the bottom, what was left of the sun's light was barely enough to see. Mike and Tim pulled out their flashlights and switched them on, holding them in their left hand while balancing their pistols in the right, ready to fire at any moment. Dust hung in the air, illuminated by the light's beams as they quickly swept across the room. There was nothing in the earthen basement, not even a mouse. The men put their guns down and quickly made their way back upstairs.

Gary and Kevin reached the northeast corner of the town and looked over the large pile of stone blocks that sat there. The rocks were cut, but had never been placed. There were enough blocks there to build a small building or start a larger one. The stone looked to be imported, not being a color that matched the rock that was local to the area.

"From the Sisseton foothills," Kevin said. "About fifty miles from here. Probably transported them by horse and carriage."

"How do you know that?" Gary asked.

"No other transportation was available to them," Kevin replied.

"No," Gary said with a laugh. "How do you know where they came from?"

"I've studied a little geology," Kevin said, "before we came here. I learned as much as I could about the area."

"At least someone did," Gary said. "Let's keep moving. The sooner we can get out of this town the better. It's giving me the creeps."

"Afraid of a little ghost?" Kevin asked.

"No," Gary replied. "But it's like; I don't know...it's weird. It's like a thousand eyes are on us here and now. I can feel them watching our every movement. It was like in high school when we were at the state finals for wrestling. Remember walking onto the mats before your match, the announcers saying your name and school, and you could feel the thousands of eyes that were watching you?"

"I remember that," Kevin said. "I know what you mean. I also remember that I won my match, but you lost yours. Pinned in the first, correct?"

"That's not the point," Gary said, snapping at him. "We're not alone here. Somebody's with us and it doesn't feel good."

"You're paranoid," Kevin said, walking toward the next structure. "There isn't anyone here so stop imagining things. And since when the hell could you feel someone's presence? You been spending too much time training with the women?"

Gary was about to reply when something caught his eye. A person, or ghost, had walked around the corner of the storage building. Both men drew their EPD guns and raced towards what Gary thought he saw. As they rounded the corner, they saw another graveyard, on the backside of the church. Where New Church had its graveyard in the front, the replica of New Church had the graveyard in the back, and where New Church's graveyard was very old, this one was brand new. The dirt on top was black and there were only four big stone markers, with many names on them.

"How many graveyards does a ghost town need?" Gary asked.

"Lots," Kevin replied. "Ya know, because people are just dying to get in."

"Ouch," Gary said. "Can we please keep the puns at least in this century?"

"That one is timeless," Kevin said. "It will never go out of style. Well, unless we unlock the key to eternity and no one dies anymore, then the subtlety of the joke would be lost on most people."

"This doesn't make sense though," Gary said looking over the ground. "All the dates on here are marked for three days ago."

"It makes perfect sense," Kevin said. "These are the residence of Whiterock, in the ultimate humiliation, buried at a mock New Church in Blackstone Hollow. Ghost Town Labs must have buried them here, along with the military men who tried to evacuate the people that night."

"This area was grass and there were no markers last week," a soft female voice said from behind them.

Kevin and Gary spun around quickly, both with their guns drawn, to see a young woman, no older than twenty-five, who instantly put her hands in the air. Both men lowered their guns as they stared at this tan woman, brunette hair in a tight bun, basic white t-shirt tied at the midriff, black capris tights, hiking boots, and a dusty backpack swung over her shoulder. She stood in a dominant, confident posture standing about five feet, ten inches tall. A hard body, thin face, and adventurous eyes made the woman look very attractive. Kevin slowly started to raise his gun again, not sure if this beauty was real, or a ghost.

Chapter #9

Jade continued to scan the area with her gun. The farm was quiet, no movement of any kind. In the town, she finally saw something, Erin and Maria heading into the school. She couldn't tell exactly what they were doing but they seemed to be in control of the situation. As Jade scanned the forest something caught her eye. It was two canoes moving slowly on the river. At first, she knew it was the red canoes of Theta Water Team, but upon further inspection Jade realized that the canoes were empty. No one was in them and they were just floating down the river. The thought frightened Jade that something might have gone that wrong. She made a mental note of it to tell Dale when he came back.

Dale slowly made his way down the stairs. He reached the base and looked over the first floor. Dale walked into the worship hall and looked at the ruins of what was left. The massive stone alter and pulpit was still standing, albeit covered in moss and vines, the same condition that the stone pews were in. Dale was stunned at the size of it, such a massive church for a small community.

As Dale walked around the sanctuary, he heard Jade's gun go off three times. He thought about heading back up to the top of the spire to see what had happened, but he didn't want to deal with her crying again. Dale knew that the ghosts could mess with a person's emotions, but he felt that Jade wasn't ready for a mission like this. Both Jade and Rachel were latecomers to the RAW Troops and he was told that only the best were being selected for this mission. It just seemed very strange to him.

As Dale pondered the structure and order of the RAW Troops, the heat finally became unbearable. Dale took his suit coat; button up shirt, and under shirt off. He set them on a pew, hoping that they could dry out before he had to put them back on. The air felt good on his bare skin, but the heat of the day was so intense that Dale didn't want to do anything. His body was getting slow and sluggish.

Dale decided to make his way into the basement. He hoped that it would be cooler down there and he could rest for a bit. Dale also thought that the basement might be a good place for ghosts to gather. Dale slowly entered the large hall where only shafts of light that broke through cracks were illuminating the room. Dale turned the tactical light at the end of his gun on and that's when his heart skipped a beat.

As the light scanned over the room Dale saw at least twenty people, all older grandma types, gathered drinking coffee and chatting. He turned the light off and they disappeared. He turned the light back on and they were there again, this time they were looking at him. Dale knew what he had to do, but to pull the trigger on a grandmother; it was something he didn't want to do. The women started to walk towards Dale so he started pulling the trigger. He shot as fast as he could and reloaded even faster. Finally, he had taken all of them out, most dispersing with only one shot, while some of them took two or three. The room was filled with mist as Dale fell to the floor and began to weep for what he had just done.

"There's no need to cry," a feminine voice said from behind him. "It was either you or the ghosts."

Dale quickly stood up and spun around. He was shocked with what he saw. A Ghost Town Labs woman, wearing the standard combat gear of a black singlet, black knee and elbow pads with black combat boots, walking towards him. To Dale's eyes, she was a goddess. She was stunningly beautiful with haunting eyes, flowing blonde hair, and a feline grace. He hadn't even heard this beauty enter the basement. Dale smiled as she approached him, trying to wipe the tears out of his eyes. He stood up straight and tried to save some face.

"Was just thinking about my grandmother," Dale said, lying. "The women I had to disperse reminded me of her."

"I'm sure they did," the woman said. "And you acted bravely, taking out the threat. You're protecting that delicate little girl in the spire too, the one with the big gun. You're like her protector, big brother. You must be very proud of yourself."

"Yeah," Dale said confused. "Who are you though? What are you doing here?"

"I'm with Ghost Town Labs," the woman said. "I'm here to thin out your numbers before you enter the lab."

"What?" Dale said as he reached for a gun that wasn't there.

"Looking for this?" the woman said, holding up Dale's Beretta. "You forgot to take it from your jacket when you took your jacket off. That's a very bad thing to do. Now, how do you want to die? Gunshot or fight?"

"Fight?" Dale asked. "You think you can kill me in a fight?"

"I've killed thousands better than you," the woman said. "I won't even break a sweat with you."

"That's what you think," Dale said before leaping into action.

Dale rushed the woman, not exactly knowing what he was going to do, but he figured the first thing would be to get her on the ground and get his gun back. The woman was still several paces away from him so he was able to build a good amount of speed before reaching her, the only problem, he project his move too far in advance. As he rushed her, she stepped to the side as she transitioned into a spinning kick that landed the steel toe of her boot into his lower abdomen.

Dale fell to his knees in a blinding pain. He was holding his stomach and trying not to scream.

The woman only had a sadistic smile on her face. Never in Dale's life had he seen someone move so quickly, so fluidly, and so precisely. The woman walked up to Dale and bowed before doing another spinning kick that landed the steel toe of her boot into Dale's throat instantly crushing his windpipe. Dale fell to the ground gasping for air. It only last for a few seconds before Dale succumbed to the pain and lack of oxygen. From only two kicks within a few seconds, the Ghost Town Labs woman had killed Dale.

The woman quickly searched through Dale's pants and coat, taking his guns and his wallet. She then moved his body to the far wall, next to Anna Tassel's casket and propped him up against it. As the woman waited, she pulled a small, black device, no bigger than a pack of gum, out of her right elbow pad. It took a few minutes, but Dale turned into a ghost. When his ghost appeared, the woman pressed a button on the top of the device and the ghost dispersed into a cloud of mist.

"Why is the large machine still running?" a female voice called out from behind her.

"Because they want more test data," the killer said. She turned around and saw her backup had entered the basement, dressed identically to her. "With all the military running around the forest, Doctor Tesla wanted to test the power of the underground separator, see how many people would be converted, and see what kind of range it had. This is the last test before we go to a big city."

"Then why didn't we just wipe out all these people the instant they got here? We had the ability to."

"I know we do, but it's not our job to question it. We just carry out the orders. All I know is that this isn't about killing people to gain power. This is revenge. This is a vendetta. Doctor Tesla wants to punish the world for what the world did to him."

"It seems like such a long way to go. He could destroy them in a day. No fighting force can stand against us."

"They made him live in fear for many years, so he will do the same to them. That's all I know about it. Come on, we have other work to do."

"What about the girl in the spire?"

"She gets to survive...for now. Another group is going to scare the daylights out of her, but they won't kill her. Same reason they didn't kill her sister."

"Why not?"

"Twins? They have a connection, a bond. Those two girls are very close to each other and would do anything to save the other. That could come in very handy for us."

"I see."

"Come on, let's move."

The two women quickly made their way back up the stairs and into the entryway of the church. They looked around and saw two ghosts starting to make their way up the stairs. The woman still had the small black device in her hand and she pushed the button on the top of it, dispersing both of the ghosts. The women then rushed to a closet and made their way inside. Behind a mass grouping of vines was a secret entrance to the lab. The killer grabbed out her keycard, swiped it, entered her code, and the door opened. They slipped out of New Church completely undetected.

Chapter #10

They continued on in silence for another ten minutes. There were many animals in and around the water, but they didn't hear anything. They didn't see anything until there was movement in the trees off the bank of the river. Larissa gave the signal to stop the canoes as she tried to see what was in the woods. The trees rustled then went still. There was no noise anywhere. No animals, no birds, no insects. Larissa swallowed hard as she raised her rifle and looked around.

Four ghosts exited the forest and stood on the banks of the river, looking at the group in the canoes. They could see through each of them. Larissa took the first shot and hit her mark. The shot hit the ghost in the chest and it instantly dispersed into mist. The next two ghosts took multiple shots each, but they both dispersed.

Larissa need to reload as the forth ghost started walking on the water towards her. Larissa looked but the other members of the group were frozen still in fear. Larissa dropped her rifle and took the pistol off her back and began to fire. She fired over ten shots and the ghost finally dispersed. Larissa breathed a sigh of relief, but instantly reloaded her guns.

When she had finished reloading, Larissa looked around to make sure there were no other ghosts in the vicinity. She thought the coast looked clear. Larissa then looked at her teammates and realized that they were all still frozen. Trey was shaking, Bradley was weeping, and Kayla was pale, white as a ghost. Larissa smiled to herself, thinking that now they might get serious.

"That," Larissa said returning the pistol to its holster, "was a ghost attack. Now you know what we are up against here, so I hope you start taking this seriously."

"But, they were ghosts," Trey said.

"I know," Larissa said. "That's what we trained to do. There's no difference in shooting them or shooting a living person. We're all trained and we have a job to do. The town of Whiterock was turned into those things."

"Could we become one of them?" Trey asked. "Could we turn into a ghost like they were?"

"Yes," Larissa said picking up her canoe paddle. "That's why we need to be alert and on our toes at all times. It can be very easy to turn us, so follow my orders. We need to keep moving."

"How do we prevent turning into one of those things?" Kayla asked picking up her oar.

"By killing them," Larissa said. "Before they kill you."

Larissa made the first few paddle strokes by herself before Kayla began to help. The men took a few more seconds to gain their wits. They rushed to catch up with the women. They continued on silently through the forest, as Larissa kept her eyes open and alert for any more movement within the trees. Eventually, they came around a bend in the river and saw the old mill.

Larissa gave the signal to shore the canoes and got out to look over the area. She took careful note of the derelict barge in the water as only Madison Tesla, a young woman who isn't a trained investigator, had investigated it. Larissa knew that she would have to be the one to look over the barge; she looked forward to it. They also needed to check over all the wagons and other ruins that were left at the mill. Larissa walked closer to the stone mill. She turned back to see that the others hadn't left the canoes yet.

"Come on," Larissa called out. "We have work to do."

"What if more of those things come?" Trey asked as they all stayed firm in the canoes. "What if they surprise us here?"

"We fight them," Larissa said. "Get your asses out of those boats, right now. We have work to do. Trey and Bradley, secure the perimeter. Use your shotguns and shoot anything that moves. Kayla, help me investigate these wagons."

"Okay," Kayla said, slowly getting out of the canoe. The others didn't move.

"Follow the order right now," Larissa said approaching the canoe. "Or I will force you out of that canoe. Come on, you cowards, move it."

Slowly, Trey and Bradley got out of the canoe. They both took their guns and walked to the edge of the forest. They stayed very close to each other as Larissa and Kayla began to investigate the wagons that had been abandoned around the mill. Larissa knew that Ethan had been over the area, but his notes were not very detailed. Larissa didn't know what to expect at the old mill, but she wanted to be detailed about it.

When Larissa was satisfied with the wagons, she walked over to the derelict barge. She motioned to Kayla to stand on the shore while she got into the water. Larissa loved being in the water. She lived for swimming and water sports throughout her childhood. She was a master diver and wished for appropriate equipment for investigating the barge, but they didn't give her anything to work with, not even a snorkel.

Larissa dove in and swam all the way to the bottom, which was only about ten feet deep, but crystal clear. The bottom of the barge rested on the riverbed, none of it was in the sandy river bottom. A lot of the bottom of the barge had rotted away, but the sidewalls were still holding strong. Larissa swam along the side nearest to the shore before she surfaced for air.

Larissa dove down again, this time along the riverside of the barge. She saw more of the same, rotted bottom and not much else to see. She was desperately hoping to see something, a Ghost Town Labs symbol, or anything that would warrant reporting. Larissa surfaced again and looked back to the shore. All looked well; the other three were watching her swim. Larissa was glad that they hadn't taken off without her.

Larissa dove again and entered the barge through a hole in the side. There was nothing inside. Most of the compartments had rotted away and there was no traces left of the flour that the ship had carried. Deciding that there were more important things to check over, Larissa swam to the surface and got out of the water.

"Anything down there?" Bradley asked.

"Nothing," Larissa said. "There was nothing there that needs reporting. Strange though, I received specific instructions that I was to investigate that barge. I was certain that there would be something in there that we needed to see."

"Who said you had to investigate it?" Kayla asked.

"It was in the orders," Larissa said. "I don't know who it came from, but they wanted to know everything about it. Give it ten years and there won't be anything left of it."

"Then we can leave this place?" Trey asked.

"Scared?" Larissa asked jokingly.

"No," Trey said harshly. "I just don't want to be here."

"That means you're scared," Larissa said. "Buck up, we've got a long day ahead of us and I can't hold your hand all day. We need to get into the mill and see what's there."

"You've got a real attitude, girl," Trey said. "Start treating us with some respect."

"I'll treat you with respect," Larissa said confronting him. "When you've earned some. So far, you've been nothing but a scared cat. I told you once, don't call me 'girl'. Do I need to remind you again?"

"The only reason you won that," Trey said. "Was because you cheated with a gun. I wasn't ready. If you want to rumble, let's go. Right now for the spot commander position of the group."

Larissa studied Trey. She was unsure of him at the start and now her fears were confirmed. Larissa had seen a memo that came out from a member of the military that had ordered RAW Troops into the field for this, one of the creators of the RAW Troops. It had warned that there might be sleepers within the group, trying to sabotage the work. Larissa knew that she was the only of the troopers in the field that had seen the note. Larissa was now certain that Trey, and possibly Bradley, were here to sabotage the work.

Larissa knew she had to act quickly. Trey was over a foot taller than her and well over one hundred pounds heavier. She knew the only reason that she bested him before was that she anticipated his reaction and was ready to pull her gun when he slammed her to the ground. In a square fight, she wouldn't have any advantage and would lose. If she walked away here then she would lose all face with the troops.

"You mean to tell me," Larissa said, thinking quickly. "That you want to jeopardize the entire mission, put everyone's lives in danger, because you're too macho to take orders from a woman? The smart man would allow me to lead, taking the point position, the most venerable spot, while you protected yourself. If I die or fail, then you take over. If we fight it out, even if you win, you lose."

"How so?" Trey asked.

"Because when we get back," Larissa said with a smile. "You will be censured and written up for disobeying orders and mutiny. You'll spend time in jail and will never be able to lead a team, if you're even allowed into the military again. That being said, let's go. Although no true military man would ever want to do this."

Larissa smiled on the inside. She knew that she just trapped Trey. If he agreed to the fight he would be admitting that he was not a true RAW Troop and here for a different reason, but she also gave him an out—a reason to back down while not losing face. She knew he would back down, but she braced herself just in case he had other orders.

"Fine," Trey finally said. "I'll follow you, but know this, if you screw up in any way, any way at all, I will report it and have you written up."

"Write me up all you want Trey," Larissa said. "Just don't call me 'girl' again."

"Okay, Larissa," Trey said. "What are the orders now?"

"Enter the mill," Larissa said.

"How?" Bradley asked. "The report said the door was stone and electronically locked."

"Did you notice some of the tools in the canoes?" Larissa asked walking towards the boats. "We need to make a door."

Larissa grabbed two pick axes and two sledgehammers from the canoes. She handed the pick axes to the men and gave one of the sledgehammers to the Kayla. They walked to the door and the men started to swing. The rock chipped away slowly and the heat was instantly taking its toll on the men. They chipped away for a bit and when there were some small holes in the door they stepped back. The women started hitting the door with the sledgehammers. The hammers rung out as they smashed against the hard rock. The women were able to make the holes a little bigger, but not by much. After a few minutes, the men started chipping again.

After a half hour of working away at the door, they were able to break it away from the lock. The door swung open and they put the tools down and picked up their EPD guns. Larissa got a flashlight out and shined it in the mill. Amazingly, it was spotlessly clean. No dust, no spider webs, nothing. Larissa slowly entered the building while the others followed.

Inside the door, there was a short hallway leading to a large room. There was a doorway on either side of the hallway with wooden doors that had long ago rotted away. One side room looked like a storage room; the other looked like a coatroom. Larissa led the way into the big, open room. On one side was an office; on the other was a large stone grinding wheel in a grinding pit. They could hear the shaft from the watermill turning, but the bearing had worn out so the wheel wasn't spinning.

The old equipment of the mill looked to be in good shape, and it looked even better since it had been recently cleaned. On the far wall, Larissa saw what she was looking for: another door with an electric lock and the Ghost Town Labs symbol above it. She rushed over to the door, but her enthusiasm was short lived when she realized the door was metal and there was no way to break it down.

"Damn," Larissa said looking over the door. "I was hoping we could see part of the lab."

"Do we have orders to enter the lab this early in the day?" Bradley asked. "I thought we were all supposed to enter at the same time."

"I had orders to enter," Larissa said. "Either here or another point on the river that we will be going to. They wanted one group to enter, do a base investigation, and get back to the group so there were some reports of the lab before the whole troop moves in."

Kayla was about to ask a question when they heard a noise behind them. The group turned around with their guns drawn and looked around. They could hear footsteps somewhere in the building, but with the stone acoustics, they couldn't tell exactly where the footsteps were coming from. They didn't have to wait long before a scrawny looking man, with long white hair, in a brown suit and white lab coat, came into view from the office of the building.

"Who the hell are you?" the man called out. "How did you get in here?"

"We are looking for someone," Larissa called out. "Who are you?"

"I work here," the man said getting closer. He looked them over. "You're nothing but a group of party kids, vandalizing government property. You're all going to jail for this."

"This isn't government property," Larissa said. "This forest is public land and this building is abandoned, but still under the ownership of the White Rock Farmers Elevator."

"That's what you think, kid," the man said. "Why do you have guns?"

"To protect ourselves," Larissa said. "Now open this door."

"No," the man said. "I'm calling the troops in here and you're all in a mess of trouble."

The man pulled a cell phone out and started to dial a number when Kayla pulled the trigger on her EPD pistol. The man screamed out as he fell to the floor and convulsed. He was human. Larissa wasted no time in firing multiple shots with her EPD pistol. After the fifth shot, the man was dead.

"It looked like he was being electrocuted," Kayla said.

"That's what an EPD shot will do to a human," Larissa said. "Hurts like hell too. About four or five shots will stop a human's heart. An autopsy would look like electrocution with some anomalies, but close enough that it wouldn't be questioned."

"Why did you kill him?" Trey asked.

"He was a threat," Larissa said, moving to the guy and taking his ID badge. "He would have called us in and that would have exposed the group."

Larissa took the badge and slid it through the card reader on the wall. A computer screen came to life and asked for a pass code. Larissa looked the badge over and took a couple guesses, punching them into the keypad but nothing opened the door. After the second time she didn't try again.

"Keep trying," Trey said.

"No," Larissa said, going back to the guy and looking him over. "I'm sure that three wrong tries would disable the system and alert any kind of security that something was wrong here. We don't need that kind of attention right now."

"What are you looking for?" Trey asked as Larissa checked the guy's pockets.

"Anything that could help us," Larissa said. "Now fan out and check over every inch of this place."

Larissa didn't find anything useful on the guy. His wallet was empty and he carried nothing else on him that would be of any use to them. Larissa slowly walked around the room, looking everything over. She noticed that Trey was constantly eyeing her and she wondered if she should take him out. She wanted to. She knew that he was just waiting to cause a problem or fight with her, but she wondered if she was wrong. What if he was just stubborn? Larissa wanted to be certain he was betraying them before she did anything.

They continued to look over the rooms when the lights by the door started to blink. They heard a clicking noise then the door opened. Larissa raised her gun up and motioned for the others to do the same. She was right to be ready. When the door opened, five ghosts entered the room. They moved with blinding speed and were hard to shoot. Larissa realized that the ghosts were trying to move in front of the other members of the team, trying to get the team to shoot each other. It took almost all the rounds they had, but they got the ghosts. When the last one died, Larissa looked at the door, but it was closed.

"Everyone," Larissa shouted out, "back to the boats and reload."

They all rushed out of the building and back to the canoes. They reloaded the guns and looked back at the building. There was no one coming out, but they waited for a moment before Larissa started heading back towards the building.

"You're not seriously going back in there?" Kayla asked. "After what just happened?"

"We're not done," Larissa said. "We need to finish looking the building over."

"Then you can do it yourself," Trey said lowering his gun. "I'm not going in there. No one said anything about ghosts when I sign up for this."

"Just a little wimp then?" Larissa asked, getting into Trey's face. "I'm giving you an order, Trey. Get in that building right now."

"You gonna make me?" Trey asked.

"If I have to," Larissa said. "I will."

Trey stared into Larissa's eyes. He smiled a smug grin before pushing her backwards. He pushed her so hard that Larissa fell over. He laughed as she hit the ground. Larissa stared back at him as he towered over her.

"It'd be wise," Trey said. "For you to stay on the ground and stay here while we get the hell out of here."

Trey turned around and started walking for the canoe. Larissa wasted no time in rolling over, lunging forward with all the force she could muster, and driving her shoulder into the back to Trey's knee. Trey fell to the ground as Larissa scrambled up and delivered a hard knee to the side of Trey's head. Trey's eyes rolled up as Larissa delivered two straight right hands to his nose. Blood gushed from his nose as Larissa rushed to her canoe. Larissa grabbed her Beretta and fired it, the bullet hitting the ground just inches from Trey's head.

"There won't be a warning shot next time," Larissa yelled. "Now get up."

"I can't," Trey said, trying to stand. "You broke my leg."

"Then you're worthless to us," Larissa said as she cocked the hammer on the gun back. "And I have to put you down so you don't hold us up."

"What?" Trey asked as he tried to stand. "Why are you doing this?"

"Tell me who you are," Larissa yelled.

"What?"

Larissa rushed him again and took Trey to the ground. She put her entire body around Trey's bad leg and twisted. Trey screamed out in pain. Larissa started hitting his knee. She was determined to rip his leg apart if he didn't start talking.

"Okay," Trey yelled. "I'm Ghost Town Labs. So is Bradley."

"What were your orders?" Larissa yelled.

"We were to destroy the operations," Trey said. "Gather as much information as we could about your team. We were to try and get you out of the area or kill you."

"I understand," Larissa said.

Larissa twisted his leg as hard as she could, and everyone winced when they heard the bones snapping. Larissa aimed her Beretta and shot Bradley in the head before he realized what was going to happen. Larissa turned the gun to Trey and drilled the barrel underneath his chin and held the gun there.

"Tell me," Larissa asked him as he squirmed in pain. "Who else is working for you?"

"Go to hell," Trey said. "Little girl."

Larissa pulled the trigger and Trey was dead.

Chapter #11

Rachel was driving a bit too fast for the narrow, winding forest road, but she wanted to put distance between her and the gruesome scene at the road's entrance. Rachel knew that the members of Gamma Ground Team would be investigating Whiterock and she knew many of the members well, having trained with some of the women before. Gamma Ground Team was made up of four women who were assigned to search for survivors. Rachel wasn't sure where in the town they would be, but she figured if she drove around she would cross paths with someone.

Rachel hardly slowed the massive Hummer down as she drove into the town. She made a hard right onto a gravel side street that led to the town hall. She thought she would start there. The dust rose off the roads on this hot July day as Rachel gunned the truck towards her destination. She slid into the parking lot sideways, brakes locked. Rachel didn't turn the truck off or close her door as she grabbed her EPD shotgun and rushed into the old town hall building.

Inside the dark, musty old building, Rachel slowly crept down a hallway trying her hardest to hear if someone else was in the building. Beads of sweat ran down her face and body, as much from her nerves as from the sweltering heat. Rachel didn't dare call out, not wanting to attract the wrong kind of attention. She slowly realized that rushing into this building may not have been the best idea. She didn't know if she would get trapped, or if one of the ghosts could sneak up from behind her. Rachel tried to move with her back to a wall and kept her eyes moving constantly.

Rachel came to a junction in the hallway and held her breath as she stuck her head around the corner. There was a ghost in the hallway. Just one and it hadn't seen her. It was a man, big and powerful looking, standing still as if he was waiting for something. Rachel looked him over. The man stood there, hands on his hips, his bald head fixed in its position. Rachel could see through him so she leveled her EPD shotgun and shot. The shot rang out inside the town hall, but he didn't disappear. Rachel quickly shot a few more times, needing six shells to take the guy down.

Rachel quickly reloaded her gun as she moved back towards the exit. She worried that the gunshot would attract more ghosts, and she was right. Six women came from different doors on the hallway. They all went down with one or two shots, but Rachel made a quick decision and ran toward the exit—she was in over her head. Rachel was almost there when a ghost appeared in her way. Rachel skidded to a stop, almost sliding through it.

At first, the ghost was a wisp of mist, not taking any real form, but then in turned into a large man. Six-foot, five inches tall, bulging, rippling muscles everywhere, arms like tree limbs, legs like tree trunks. He wore dirty denim overalls with no shirt underneath, stringy brown hair, and a beard in desperate need of a trim. His hauntingly piercing eyes almost seemed to hypnotize Rachel. Before Rachel knew it, the man was solid, so solid that if she hadn't seen him materialize in front of her she would have thought he was real.

Rachel unloaded the six shells in her shotgun, but they had no effect. The ghost only laughed at her. Rachel pulled her EPD pistol and shot fifteen more rounds into the ghost, which stunned him, forced him to his knees, and allowed Rachel to reload her shotgun. Rachel was about to shoot him with the shotgun when something she wasn't ready for happened; the ghost talked to her.

"You think you can win?" the ghost said with a taunting tone. "You think that your little guns and weapons will work on all of us? You people are so easy to kill. We can sense your fear; we know exactly where you are. You will all die here."

Rachel wasted no time in unloading the shotgun on him again, and this time, he vanished into mist. She turned around to see three more ghosts moving towards her. She quickly put a new clip into her pistol and dispersed them. Rachel took a deep breath to compose herself and reloaded all her guns and magazines before left the building.

Rachel sat in the Hummer, wondering where to go next. She thought of the churches in Whiterock, the main buildings, the general store, or the elevator—all places where Gamma team could be searching. Rachel strained to think back to the briefing that took place. She'd been in the simulator when the call came in. She was battling multiple computer systems and other planners as they were waging war against each other. Rachel knew of all the variables that go into planning, and how fast they can all go to hell, but for the first time in a long time, she felt alone. She knew there were troops somewhere in this town, but she felt like there was no one here to protect her. Rachel began to cry.

Rachel cried as hard as she could, as she felt sorry for herself and the situation she'd gotten into. She thought of her teammates, dead in the ravine, the cops, burned in the cars, and that's when Rachel realized that there was a ghost nearby. She wasn't some soft, weak, pathetic crybaby. Rachel chambered a shell into the shotgun, wiped her tears, and got out of the truck. She looked around and saw a teenage girl by the rear of the Hummer, talking on a cell phone. Two bullets later and the girl was gone. Rachel felt a whole lot better.

Rachel was stunned that her emotions could have been so greatly affected, but the ghost had given her an idea. Rachel reached into her shorts pocket for her cell phone; she would just call Kelly, the spot commander for Gamma Ground Team. Rachel felt foolish for not thinking of that earlier, but she quickly had a new concern—her phone wasn't in her back pocket.

Rachel checked her other pockets before jumping into the Hummer and searching every square inch of it. That's when it hit her; Rachel had been wearing a sleeveless button up shirt this morning and had had the phone in the chest pocket. Rachel punched the dash in frustration realizing that the shirt was hanging on a tree back at their original location.

Rachel scolded herself as harshly as she could for forgetting the phone. She thought she should have known better than to not keep it on her person at all times. Rachel realized that her only option now was to drive around and hope to find someone else in the town. Rachel slammed the door to the Hummer shut and pushed her foot to the floor, causing the heavy truck to fishtail as it sped out of the parking lot. Rachel tore down the streets of Whiterock, blasting the horn, hoping someone would see her. Rachel passed house after house, not seeing anyone until some minor movement caught her eye.

Rachel whipped the Hummer around and drove right onto the lawn, knocking over the picturesque white picket fence and locked the brakes up as she came to a stop. Shotgun in hand, Rachel rushed to the door, but stopped on the porch, not wanting to repeat what had happened at the town hall. Rachel called out and knocked on the door but no one replied. Rachel looked around until she heard laughter behind her. Rachel spun around to see two little kids playing on the porch, in a spot she had just looked at not seconds before and it had been empty. Rachel dispatched the kids with one bullet each before she pumped more shells into her gun.

Rachel peered into the house from one of the windows. Everything inside was destroyed. It looked like a tornado had gone through there. She could see mist moving around the house, but nothing had taken shape or form. Rachel thought about moving on when she saw Maria Diego walking in the house. Rachel quickly rushed into the house, making sure to leave the door open. Rachel called out for Maria, but she didn't stop. Rachel rushed into the kitchen of the house and stopped dead in her tracks.

Maria, the swords and knife expert of RAW Troops, was in a face off with a ghost. The ghost was nondescript; a blob of mist hanging in the air, but it seemed menacing and threatening. Rachel raised her gun and shot twice, dispensing the mist. Two more ghosts appeared and Rachel used the rest of the shells in her shotgun to take them out. She turned back to Maria and Maria changed into a different form: a mid-forties blonde woman in a business suit. Rachel was stunned; she'd been led into a trap. The ghost lured her into the house by posing as a member of the team and got her to use her shotgun shells up on other ghosts.

The woman took two steps towards Rachel before Rachel pulled out her EDP pistol and open fired, unloading all fifteen shots into the woman. The woman disappeared into the air, but not in the same manner as other ghosts did when they were dispersed. As Rachel put a new magazine into her pistol, she rushed towards the door, which was shut tight and locked. She fumbled with the knob, but realized that the handle was broken and she couldn't get out. Rachel took a couple steps back and rushed the door, but her weight was no match for the heavy door and she fell back to the ground.

Rachel had the wind knocked out of her, so it took her a few moments before she could stand up. As Rachel was getting up, she noticed the woman coming towards her from down the hall. Rachel unloaded another fifteen rounds from the EPD pistol and the woman disappeared again, but

Rachel wasn't sure if she was gone for good. She took her Beretta pistol out and shot out the lock on the door as she stood and rushed the door again. This time the door flew open before she hit it and Rachel went flying outside, losing her balance, and falling down the steps of the house.

The landing on the cement sidewalk hurt and she was sure she'd be bruised, but she saw the woman coming at her again. Rachel scrambled to the Hummer and opened the back door, grabbing Blake's EPD shotgun. Rachel unloaded that, then Jake's, then the other EPD guns she had. Rachel finally watched the ghost disperse in the air. Rachel wasted no time in getting in the Hummer and tearing out of there.

Rachel slammed the pedal to the floor and raced out of town towards the Tesla farm. Rachel knew the tactical commander was there and she would know what to do. Rachel was traveling at over one hundred miles an hour when she reached the first curve in the road. Rachel slammed on the brakes and it took all the control and ability she had not to lose control of the truck. Rachel decided that a safer speed would be more advisable on the narrow, winding forest road.

She finally saw the entrance to the Tesla farm and she drove in, bringing the Hummer up to the house, before shutting it off. In the initial reports, it said that there were no ghosts reported at the farm and Rachel hoped that was true. She didn't know how much trouble she'd be in for losing her phone and abandoning her post, but after what she'd seen, Rachel didn't care. A black military Hummer was parked in the yard, but there weren't any people around. Rachel hoped she'd find someone.

Chapter #12

The noise of the breaking window perked Kelly and Brady up. They were running towards the school, close to where they heard the noise. They saw Maria and Erin jumping out the window so both Kelly and Brady took knees, aiming EPD guns at the broken window as the other girls ran past them. When Erin had passed, and no ghosts came out of the window, Kelly and Brady got up and ran with the others. The girls ran until they were in an open playing field where they all sat down, back to back, to make sure nothing could sneak up on them.

"What happened in there?" Kelly asked.

"Sorry, Commander," Maria said. "We got trapped."

"Trapped?" asked Brady.

"Trapped," Erin said. "Meaning the ghosts set a trap for us to lure you in there as well. These things are good, and convincing. I didn't even realize they were ghosts. How did you figure it out Maria?"

"Look in their eyes," Maria said. "They can look perfect on the outside, but the eyes are empty, with a mist in them. It's the only way to tell on the higher classes of ghost."

"How many were in there?" asked Kelly.

"We were chased by a large group, Commander," Maria said. "At least twenty, maybe more."

"Why didn't you respond to the checks?" asked Brady.

"Lost our packs," Erin said looking in hers. "All they left us was our phones. Either of you have any water?"

"No," Kelly said. "Here's the plan, we're useless without supplies. I wouldn't be any good right now in a fight, and I think we're all in the same boat. We need water. The town is fed by artesian wells, meaning that there's no need for filtration and the power's still running so we should be able to find edible food. The general store is at the end of Main Street and the fastest way there is through the cemetery."

All the girls were quiet. None of them had felt courageous enough to go through the cemetery yet. They had all done their best to avoid it. They could deal with the other places, but to be above the dead, they thought, would be pressing their luck.

"The cemetery?" Erin asked.

"There's nothing to fear," Kelly said. "In fact, that's most likely the safest place."

"And how in the world do you figure that?" asked Brady.

"Think for a second," Kelly said. "These things had to change when they were living, nobody living in a graveyard. It's not like the corpses are going to jump out of the ground and try to eat us. Plus, maybe they can't enter a holy place."

"What evidence do you base that on?" Erin asked.

"Nothing," Kelly said with a smile. "But we can hope right? Now everyone up and follow me, guns at the ready, Maria, you bring up the rear."

The group stood and followed Kelly as she rushed along a fence line that led away from the school. They quickly came in sight of the church and cemetery, which were both eerily quiet. The group cautiously approached the gates and scanned the area as Kelly opened the gate and slowly made her way inside. Kelly and the team moved quickly, staying close to the fence in case they had to get out, but there was no movement.

Kelly knew from the briefings that when one of the ghosts was near it could affect you, but she felt fine, and none of her team was showing any signs of strangeness. Kelly hadn't agreed with the rule not to tell the team what they were up against, so she made sure they met some ghosts as quickly as they could, within fifteen minutes of them arriving in Whiterock. It was a short encounter, a group of ghost kids, but it got the point across.

They kept running and upon arriving to the other side of the cemetery, they could see the general store, but they could also see six ghosts by the entrance. Kelly used her rifle to disperse the ghosts, noting that they were all shadows, needing two or three shots to take out, so she was glad her rifle had a large magazine. They waited for a moment to see if more ghosts would arrive, but none did, so they rushed into the store.

It was hotter inside than outside. The girls wasted no time in each grabbing a bottle of water and drinking it down. The water was cold and refreshing. The women were glad to get it. Erin took a cooler from the shelf and filled it with water bottles, granola bars, and jerky. She looked over to see Brady eating a chocolate bar, her one weakness, as Kelly was looking over the shoe selection. There wasn't many, but Kelly took off her boots and put on a pair of men's sneakers. The shoes were much more comfortable than the boots, and more practical.

With their cooler and canteen's full, the girls looked over the rest of the meager selections of the store. Hunting knives, a compound bow, various arrows, food, bait, clothes, tools, and household items. Everything was five years out of date and dusty. Kelly went behind the counter, looking over what was there. She noticed that the other girls had their guns raised in alarm and Kelly then realized that she had put chewing tobacco in her mouth. She was still holding onto the tin, not even remembering picking it up.

Kelly raised her rifle as they all scanned the area. There was no movement anywhere, no mist hanging in the air. Erin was the first to see it; a group of about ten teenagers entered the store. They were talking and laughing like all was right with the world. The girls wasted no time in opening fire. It took multiple shots for each of the shadows. When the last one had dispersed, the girls breathed a sigh of relief. Kelly spit the tobacco out of her mouth and rinsed her mouth out with a bottle of water from one of the coolers.

"That's attractive," Brady said smiling. "What's our next move, Commander?"

"I don't really know," Kelly said, spitting some more. "I think the original plan of being split up is too dangerous, considering what you saw in the school. If these things are smart, then we need to stick together. I think we should get back to our Hummer, drive it to the open field, and post on the roof of the truck."

"I have a suggestion," Erin said meekly.

"What's that?" Kelly asked.

"We need to burn the school down," Erin said. "With the power of those two we saw there, who knows what else is there, but we saw a lot of them and none of them left the school when we left."

"I know how we could do it," Brady said. "Look over there, four propane tanks. We put them in a room with a closed window, open the valves, let them bleed out for a couple minutes, then shoot a flaming arrow into the room. It will be one hell of an explosion."

"It would kill anyone near it," Maria said.

"If we put it in a room with a window facing the church," Brady said. "I could shoot it from the bell tower."

"You a good enough shot?" Kelly asked.

"I went bow hunting with my dad and brothers every year," Brady said. "Bagged my first deer when I was thirteen. Won the year too with a ten pointer."

"Okay," Kelly said. "Erin, come with me. We each grab two tanks and fill them up. Brady and Maria, get whatever you need to bring that building down."

"You grab the bow and arrows," Maria said to Brady as Kelly and Erin walked outside with the tanks. "I'll get the matches and lighter fluid. Need to make sure these arrows will burn."

Kelly held the small propane tank to the fill hose. Although she had reservations about what they were about to do, she couldn't help but wonder what the explosion was going to look like. In the briefing, they told her that fire destroyed these things, so technically they were following orders. Once they had the tanks full, they waited for the others to get out. Brady exited the store first, holding the compound bow with a quiver of arrows slung on her back. Maria followed carrying a can of lighter fluid and a bag full of matches and cigarette lighters.

The group followed Kelly as she quickly rushed back towards the school. They didn't waste any time in getting to the building. Once there, they found an open window that led into a small room. They scanned the room from the outside and when they were sure it was safe Kelly and Maria boosted Erin into the room. They handed her the tanks and she carried them, one by one, to the far wall. Erin opened the valves on each tank before rushing out of the room. They closed the window behind her when something startled them.

The group could hear a car horn honking. They moved away from the school building, somewhat making their way towards the church, but looking for what was going on. None of them could imagine who would be in the town with a car right now. As they were almost back to the church, they saw the Beta Watch Team's

Hummer, being driven by Rachel Chance, tearing out of town.

"That was Rachel Chance," Kelly said. "I didn't see Blake or Jake with her. Odd."

"What was she doing here?" Brady asked. "They're supposed to be at the entrance to the road."

"Brady, Maria, wait here at the graveyard," Kelly said. "Erin and I are going to check out where she came from. The way she was driving she looked scared to death."

Kelly and Erin rushed around the corner in the direction that Rachel came from as Brady and Maria waited in the graveyard. They were keeping a close eye on what was going on around them but there was nothing. Brady made her way to the front of the church, by the doors and underneath an overhang, so she was out of the sun. Brady took the bow and got it into position. She pulled an arrow from the quiver and loaded it. Brady picked a car a block away and aimed for the front tire. She released the arrow and hit her mark perfectly. She was about to shoot another one when Kelly and Erin returned, running at top speed with ten ghosts chasing them.

Brady and Maria quickly grabbed their guns and began firing on the ghosts. They were luckily able to shoot all of them before any ghosts got into the cemetery. Kelly and Erin stopped by the door, flushed, sweating, and out of breath.

"That was a close one," Kelly said, still gasping for air. "There were a lot of them. Rachel must have met up with them."

"We got them," Maria said. "Let's get inside."

The group quickly rushed inside the wooden church and they all rushed up to the bell tower. From the top of the bell tower, they had an amazing view of the city. It looked so nice down there. They couldn't see any ghosts, anything of the tragedy that had befallen this place. Brady put a pair of heavy, brown leather gloves on before dousing the longest arrow in lighter fluid. She hoped it would stay lit the entire way to the school. Brady loaded the arrow and sighted it in. She slowed her breathing, imagining that she was lining up on the perfect twelve-point buck, needing to shoot it before her brothers get it. Brady nodded to Maria, who lit a match and touched the arrow tip with it, which ignited in a strong flame.

The other women ducked down beneath the wall of the tower as Brady pushed everything else out of her mind. She was focused solely on this shot. Brady let the arrow loose and quickly ducked beneath the wall, just in time as a roar ripped through the town. The women could see a fireball rising above the bell tower and wood chunks were falling everywhere. The women looked over the wall to see the school in a raging inferno. It was an amazing sight to see and the women could feel the heat coming off the building.

"That was great," Erin said. "Except for we forgot one thing."

"What?" Kelly asked.

"That it's been so dry," Erin continued. "That all the houses and buildings are starting to burn, including this church."

Kelly looked and realized that Erin was right. Some debris that was still on fire had landed on the roof of the church and the building was starting to burn. No one said anything as the women quickly gathered their supplies and raced down the stairs. They exited the church, back into the cemetery, and looked back. The fire started to flash over to the church; the wood was so dry it went up like kindling. Many houses around the school were also going up.

Kelly motioned and the other women followed as they rushed through the town. Kelly led them to the black Hummer that they'd arrived in. They jumped in and Kelly raced the big truck to the big open grass field on the south edge of town. The girls got out and got on top of the truck. They had one looking each way, with Brady looking directly at the fire that was destroying a portion of the town.

"I pray that there were no people hiding in those buildings," Brady said. "I really hope they were empty."

"If there were any people left," Maria said. "They'd have been dead by now."

"Or else the explosion would have gotten their attention," Kelly said. "And they would have been able to get out."

"What's the plan now?" Erin asked. "I mean, what do we do?"

"We have some options," Kelly said. "We could post here, finish out the mission watching from here, and wait for the chopper, or we could stick together and search the houses and buildings that haven't caught fire."

"There's not going to be any houses left, Commander," Maria said.

"What?" Kelly asked.

"With the breeze we have?" Maria asked rhetorically. "Considering weather patterns around here, the wind picks up to about ten miles an hour at night. That fire will spread. The only thing left is going to be the cement elevator; everything else in this town is going to burn—"

Maria cut off, her mouth hanging open in disbelief. The others looked to see what she saw and they were all stunned. Four large Oshkosh fire trucks were arriving on the scene. The crews were working fast to extinguish the fires. A mist was coming out of the hoses, putting the fires out quickly. Ghosts were operating everything. Some of them were dispersing from getting too close to the fires but most were being careful to stay a safe distance away. The women had all gotten their guns at the ready in case something happened as they watched the efficient crew of ghosts putting out the fire.

Chapter #13

"State your name," Kevin said with a bark. "And your business here."

"Sara," Sara replied. "I'm Sara James. I come out here once in a while to visit my ancestors. It makes me feel connected to them. I came out here to write about them. Mainly fiction, but I base it on what really happened here. Most soap operas today couldn't match the drama of Whiterock and Blackstone Hollow. What are you two doing here?"

"You haven't heard?" Gary asked. "About the accident at the Tesla farm and the destruction of Whiterock?"

"My gosh," Sara said in horror. "When did that happen?"

"A couple days ago," Kevin said. "I'm really sorry, ma'am. I would have loved to have gotten to know you, but, we can't take the risk."

Kevin pulled up his EPD gun and pulled the trigger. It hit Sara in the stomach. She let out a blood curdling scream and doubled over, grabbing her stomach in pain. She fell to the ground crying, and she shook for a moment as if she was being electrocuted. Finally, the charge stopped, but Sara remained on the ground, crying out in pain.

"What was that?" Sara asked through her tears. "How could you do something like that to me?"

"I'm sorry," Kevin said. "I thought you were a ghost. I know that sounds impossible, but we've killed ghosts in the forest today. We've seen people vanish in front of our eyes, after we could see right through them. We couldn't take the risk that you'd turn on us. A scientist's machine is what's causing all the problems here. It's what killed all the people in Whiterock. Again, so sorry."

Kevin helped Sara up while Gary got out some food and water for her. She took the water, but refused the food. Kevin helped her over to a pile of wood and got her to sit down. The entire time Sara was holding her stomach, her face flushed and she was shaking.

"How do you feel?" Kevin asked, sitting next to her.

"Weak," Sara replied. "Very weak, like I was electrocuted. What the hell was that thing?"

"It's an electro-plasma distorter," Kevin replied. "The only way, other than fire, that can kill a ghost."

"Kill a ghost?" Sara asked skeptically.

"Okay, not kill the ghost," Kevin said. "But get rid of them, banish them from this plain of existence, disperse them. We have military troops all over the area. How did you get in here without running into any of them?"

"I have a secret entrance," Sara said lifting her shirt to look at the mark on her stomach where the charge hit. "It's at the north edge of the forest. I drive down a field road to get there then this place is only about a twenty minute hike down a trail."

"So you were never on the old forest road?" Gary asked. "You never saw any of our posts?"

"None," Sara replied. "I don't know anyone from Whiterock. I'm a descendant of some of the original members of Blackstone Hollow though. There was some bad blood between the families here. I come here to get away, write, and be at peace. It's hard to find that in a big city."

"Well, I'd love to stay and chat," Kevin said getting up. "But we have to search these ground then make our way to a secret lab underneath the forest. It would be best for you to get away from here as quickly as possible, Sara. Don't stop for anything or anyone. Give me your phone number so I can contact you when this is over to make sure you got home safely."

"Yeah," Sara said laughing. "That's not going to happen. I give you points for trying, but I don't give my number to guys who shoot unarmed girls without asking any questions first. Not a good trait."

"Either way," Gary said. "You have to leave."

"Fine," Sara said standing up. "I will leave. Have fun hunting ghosts, boys."

Sara started walking away. Kevin watched her until she was out of sight. He smiled, wishing she would have given him her number, but he knew that he had to get his mind focused on what they were doing. Kevin and Gary began to scan the grounds some more. They walked over the fresh graves of the Whiterock people and looked for any other signs. They walked around some decrepit houses that were nothing more than foundations and rotting wood.

Kevin and Gary investigated more houses and buildings, being very careful to not enter any of them. Kevin noted that it had been a long time since they'd seen a ghost or had to shoot anything, but he figured that since they were so deep in the forest there wouldn't be of them lurking about. They noticed that Mike and Tim had entered the gallery area between the church and town hall. Kevin and Gary walked over to them.

"Find anything?" Mike asked.

"A woman," Kevin said. "Someone doing some writing. We sent her on her way."

"You sure she wasn't a ghost?" Tim asked.

"Yeah," Kevin replied. "She didn't take to kindly to me when I shot her with an EPD."

"That had to hurt," Mike said. "What did she do then?"

"We explained what was going on," Kevin said. "Then she left. She agreed to stay away."

Mike was about to ask another question when they heard a woman scream. She was screaming at the top of her lungs, coming from the grain storage building. The guys quickly rushed towards the building, guns all drawn, ready to fire. They entered the stone building and headed down the long hallway. They reached the doors and there was only one open.

Mike led the way into the room and the others followed, only to find Sara in a chair, tied up with her back to the door. The men paused, trying to assess the situation. Kevin rushed to Sara and untied her.

"Are you hurt?" Kevin asked. "What happened?"

"Some women," Sara said. "They caught me as I tried to leave the area and they brought me here and tied me up. I have no idea why. I wasn't able to get a look at them."

"Where did they go?" Mike asked.

"I couldn't see," Sara said. "I had my back to the door, but I did hear them leave. That's when I started to scream, hoping that you would hear me and come for me."

"You're safe now, Sara," Kevin said. "I promise you that you're safe. I'll stay here with

Sara while you three check the rest of this building."

"Okay," Mike said as he and the others headed out the door.

Kevin was unsure about what to do or say, but he checked over the empty room. He looked around near the door and in the corners of the room. There was nothing there and Kevin felt scared, truly scared, for the first time today. He didn't know what was going on or what was happening.

"Come here," Sara said, motioning to Kevin. "I need someone to hold me."

"Of course," Kevin said with a big smile.

"First thing though," Sara said holding up her hands. "Take your guns off. I don't trust you yet. Put them on the floor in the corner."

Kevin thought about it for a moment, but Sara was standing seductively and he could imagine the things they were about to do. He knew there was only one way into the room and that there were three other military men about. Kevin thought that he would be safe. Kevin took the guns off and placed them in the corner before walking towards Sara. Kevin took his shirt off and tossed it back towards his guns as he approached her.

"You'll be safe with me," Kevin said.

"I know I'll be safe," Sara said. "Just looking at you I know I'll be safe."

Chapter #14

While Jade was listening to the rapid gunfire in the basement, she had to shoot at two more men who were on the edge of the farmyard. She thought it would be much easier to pull the trigger if these people weren't looking directly at her. Every time she met with a ghost's eyes, she felt her blood chill. It wasn't a feeling that she liked.

After a few moments of quiet, she wondered if Dale was okay or if he needed some help. She thought that she could hear voices, but there were so many strange noises out here and she didn't pay much attention to them. Jade figured that Dale was competent and could handle anything. If she couldn't be placed with her sister, she was glad to be put with someone as good as Dale. As Jade scanned the yard again, she heard footsteps coming up the stairs. Jade quickly grabbed her EPD pistol and pointed at the doorway, hoping it would only be Dale coming up instead.

Jade was stunned when a teenage girl, six feet tall and thick, with solid muscle being held in a one-piece lifeguard swimsuit entered the spire.

Pixy cut brown hair gave way to a round face with hazel eyes and a sharp nose. The girl was as stunned as Jade was. She instantly put her hands in the air.

"Please help me," the girl said with desperation in her voice. "I need someone to help me."

"Who are you?" Jade asked slowly lowering the gun, getting no indications that this girl was a ghost. "And what are you doing here?"

"My name is Kyrie Hamilton," Kyrie said. "I escaped Whiterock when the people started turning into those demons and I ran to my boyfriend's fort. We use to hang out there and stuff. He was going to get his little sister and meet me there, but they never showed up."

"Tell me everything," Jade said as she slowly inched closer to Kyrie. "Everything that happened from the first time you saw one of those things until you got here. But first."

Jade slowly inched up to Kyrie, keeping the pistol aimed at her, and she poked her with the barrel of the gun, first in the chest, then in the stomach. When Jade was sure Kyrie was human, she hugged her.

"You're solid," Jade said putting the pistol away. "Now tell me everything."

"I had just gotten done with my shift at the swimming pool," Kyrie said. "My boyfriend Matt had been swimming with his friends and his little sister was there with some of her friends. Matt was walking me home when we heard a commotion. We saw the military trying to get people into some buses. They were saying that there was an attack in the area and they had to get us out of there. That's when these women showed up. They shot everyone, but they all came back as ghosts. Matt told me to run to the fort and hide while he went and got his sister. I started running and turned back to see Matt get shot by one of those women."

"I'm so sorry," Jade said interrupting.

"Thanks," Kyrie continued. "I ran through a store and heard someone yelling for me, I don't know exactly what they were saying but I didn't stop, I ran as fast and as hard as I could and I made it to the fort. I got in, fastened a board over the trap door entrance, and curled up into a ball and started crying. I cried and cried for I don't know how long. Before I left, I saw my parents as those things. My brother was one of them. I was so scared. I didn't dare leave the fort. We use to eat there sometimes, but there were only empty cans. Please, I haven't eaten in three days. Do you have anything you could spare?"

"Of course," Jade said.

Jade handed Kyrie some beef jerky and a bottle of water from her bag. Kyrie wasted no time devouring the food. As Kyrie ate, Jade made a scan of the farm. She had to shoot two women. Jade did another scan of the yard then a scan of Whiterock, where she saw Gamma Ground Team running into a church graveyard. She watched them for a moment, but when Kyrie started talking she turned her attention back to her.

"Anyway," Kyrie said. "I didn't know what to do. I thought about killing myself, after what I'd seen, I didn't see the point in living. Then I decided that I didn't want to take the coward's way out. I figured I would just have to starve to death. I didn't imagine anyone coming out here again. When I heard your gunshots, I decided I had to try. I had to find out what was going on here."

"You've been through so much," Jade said giving Kyrie another hug. "How old are you?"

"Seventeen." Kyrie replied.

"Oh my gosh," Jade said stunned. "You're big for your age. I'm sorry, that came out wrong. I mean you're attractive, but very tall for a teenager."

"I get it," Kyrie said. "Everyone in my family is tall and athletic. Can you help me?"

"I can and will," Jade said. "We have a chopper that will be bringing in a team soon. I can get you out with them. You'll have to hang out here with my partner and me until we get the signal to head for the farm."

"Speaking of you partner," Kyrie said. "I heard all the shots he took when I was walking in, and then I heard him crying. I think he started to talk to someone after that."

"It's these things," Jade said. "They mess with your mind and your emotions. I haven't been this confused and upset since I was thirteen. It's a real pain. I was told that they're pure energy, which lets them do things to you."

"What are these things?" Kyrie asked. "How does someone turn into a ghost?"

"There's a machine," Jade said. "A device that was funded by the government in an effort to create a new warrior, someone who couldn't be killed. Whiterock was the testing grounds for the first open run of this machine. It was created by Doctor Tesla."

"Victor?" Kyrie interrupted.

"Yes," Jade replied. "Victor Tesla, you know him?"

"I knew his daughter Madison," Kyrie said. "I kind of hated her."

"Why?"

"She always beat me out in sports," Kyrie said. "A lot of girls hated her for that. Madison took my spot on the volleyball and basketball teams. She was an amazing athlete though. I was just glad she was on our team. I got into a boxing match with her once; it was something we did around here on the weekends to pass the time. Got my ass kicked. Madison had the best record out of any of the kids in the area. I never knew much about her father though, other than his name. I don't think I'd ever seen him. He never came to any of our games."

"Well," Jade said, "he was the one to create the device. I believe it's called a separator. It separates the soul from the body. He was working for the government, in a secret division, but he took it private, and is trying to use it for his own ends. The company now controlling this technology is called Ghost Town Labs."

"Ghost Town Labs?" Kyrie asked. "You know, I've heard of Ghost Town Labs. There was a rumor about an abandoned building in the forest with a lock on it that was marked Ghost Town Labs."

"I'm sure it was true," Jade said. "We know of a few of them out there."

"I see," Kyrie said. "So, how long until this chopper gets here?"

"Could be hours," Jade said.

"The thing is," Kyrie said. "I've been in that fort for three days now and I didn't have any change of clothes, only this swimsuit. I had my cover ups but since it was so hot that night I'd just left them in my bag, which I lost when I was running into the forest. Do you have anything I could change into?"

"I don't think I would have anything that would fit you," Jade said, digging into a duffel bag. "But between my partner and I we should have something you could wear."

From the bag, Jade handed Kyrie a black t-shirt and a pair of red gym shorts that belonged to Dale, and a tank top and running shorts that belonged to her. Kyrie turned around and took the swimsuit off. Jade watched as Kyrie put the tank top and running shorts on. Jade laughed to herself. On Jade, they would be slightly too big, on Kyrie, they looked like underwear, which is what she used them as, putting Dale's shirt and shorts on over. Jade took another look through the scope while Kyrie adjusted her outfit. The yard was quiet.

"I mean no offense," Kyrie said walking up to Jade. "And I do thank you for your help, but aren't you a little young, and a lot girly to be a military sniper?"

"None taken," Jade said with a smile. "I have a twin sister and we thought this would be something good for us. Neither of us knew what we wanted to do, and we've always been very close, so we thought a tour in the military together would give us some experience and let us figure things out."

"No clue what you wanted to do?" Kyrie asked.

"Well, we had a plan," Jade said with a sigh. "But last year we were both cut in the final qualifying round for the Olympic Gymnastics team. That's all we'd trained for our entire childhood. We had no clue and everyone always thought, as you put it, that we were both very girly, so we thought this would be a good way to break the mold and get us some experience. What were your plans?"

"Interesting choice," Kyrie said. "Matt's family farmed and he had joined the family business. Matt was a year older than I am. He had graduated this past spring. He was going to farm and we were going to get married the weekend after I graduated. This would have been my senior year at school. My family farms too so I would have helped out, and we would have had lots of cattle, and lots of kids. We both wanted a lot of kids."

"That's a good plan," Jade said.

"It's gone now," Kyrie said with a tear in her eye. "Like my parents, siblings, Matt, and everything else I ever knew and loved. It's all gone, and why? Some military experiment? What kind of life is this? Will Whiterock ever be the same again?"

"I don't know Kyrie," Jade said. "You will be safe with us. I'll get you to safety. From there, I have no answers for you."

Kyrie was trying to be strong, but she cracked and started to cry. Jade tried to comfort her, but it wasn't working. Kyrie buried her head deep into Jade's shoulder and let it all out. All the pain and fear for everyone and everything she'd loved and lost. Jade was beginning to worry that it had been so long since she'd heard anything of Dale, and she didn't know how he would take to Kyrie being with them, but Jade knew this girl needed to be around someone. Kyrie suddenly pulled away from Jade and looked around the forest.

"It's always been very beautiful up here," Kyrie said. "Matt and I would hike through the forest on dates. I had my first kiss with him in this tower. I drank my first beer in this tower."

"I've never seen anything like it," Jade said going back to her scope. "The forest here is wonderful. So much diversity, so many animals, it really is a magical place."

"It's far too quiet though," Kyrie said. "There are so many animals out there that should be making noise; I don't know why we can't hear them."

"The animals must be scared too," Jade said.

Jade was about to continue when they heard footsteps coming up the stairs. Jade perched on one knee with her gun aimed at the doorway, while Kyrie got behind her. They had to wait a moment, but three ghosts, all men in their mid-thirties, came through the door. Jade needed four shots for each of them, but they all dispersed into mist. Jade quickly reloaded her EPD pistol and waited, but no more ghosts appeared.

"You know how to use a gun?" Jade asked.

"Please, I'm a farm girl," Kyrie replied. "I was shooting guns before I could spell 'gun'."

"Okay," Jade said digging in the duffel bag. She pulled out another EPD pistol and handed it to

Kyrie. "This is an Electro-Plasma Distorter. It's the only way we know of to get rid of the ghosts, other than fire. We're going to search the grounds and see where Dale went. He's been gone for far too long and I want to know what's going on. Follow me and stay close."

Jade was about to leave the spire when a huge explosion rocked the town of Whiterock. Jade tossed Kyrie the binoculars while she looked in her scope. Both girls scanned the town, looking at the school that was on fire. They were searching for anybody, any indication as to what caused the school to blow.

Chapter #15

Larissa looked over the mill and the mayhem that just took place. She was amazed at how quickly things took a turn. She knew that the reason that she got the warning was that she would have traitors in her group. She wasn't sure that if she hadn't gotten that warning if she would have put it together so quickly. Larissa quickly stood up and turned her Beretta to Kayla.

"Look me in the eyes," Larissa said. "And tell me exactly who you are. Believe me Kayla; I'll know if you're lying to me."

"Larissa," Kayla said. "I am who I say I am. I'm Kayla Johnson, RAW Troops member. What you don't know about me is that I'm not a military expert or athletes like everyone else. I'm a scientist who's here to figure out the science behind the separators. I promise you, that's who I am."

"I believe you," Larissa said lower her gun. "I knew you had more of a reason to be here. We need to get out of here. Get their weapons."

Larissa reloaded her Beretta before pushing both canoes into the water. She took a rope from her bag and tied one canoe behind the other.

Larissa held the canoes in position until Kayla got to them and got in the front one. Larissa took the front position in the front canoe and they started to paddle, pulling the second canoe behind them.

When they got out of sight of the mill, Larissa pulled out her GPS device and looked over the river system. She knew there were a number of forks coming up and she didn't want to get lost. They still had a number of sights to look at, but down to only two members they wouldn't be able to do everything they were supposed to cover.

"Are we going to continue on alone?" Kayla asked. "Or should we find another group to join up with?"

"We have our work to do," Larissa said. "Just as they do. We are far away from everyone right now."

"We could be to Blackstone Hollow," Kayla said. "In about twenty minutes. We could wait for Delta Forest Team. Or we could be at New Church in about an hour, meet up with Jade and Dale."

"We need to do our work," Larissa said. "I just hope that everyone understands what happened out there. I just wonder who else is working for Ghost Town Labs?"

"Who knows how high up it goes," Kayla said. "This whole mission could have been a setup for us."

"I know," Larissa said. "I've got the route now. Let's go."

The two began to paddle again, moving swiftly down the river. When they reached points where the river split, Larissa expertly navigated the canoes down the river. At a point with rocks, the girls had to get out and carry the canoes in the water. The trees grew to the edge of the river and the water was too shallow to float the canoes. Larissa had planned for this, and thought that the men would have carried the canoes. Larissa and Kayla made it, but it was a struggle.

As they paddled along, Larissa noticed ghosts through the trees. They hadn't noticed them yet and she motioned to Kayla to get out of the canoe. The water was about four feet deep and the ghosts were to the right of them. The girls got on the left side of the boat and held onto it as they walked along. They ducked down so that none of the ghosts on the right side of the river could see them.

Larissa swam under the boat and tried to look at what was on the right side the river. The sight made her heart skip a beat. There were at least fifty ghosts standing there. She got back to the other side, praying that they didn't see her. The girls continued along in the water, around the bend, and further down the river before Larissa looked on the right side again. There were no ghosts standing there now, but they moved along in the water until they were past another bend.

Larissa realized that they were at the next point they were supposed to investigate. She grabbed a rope from the canoe and tied it to a tree that was near the water's edge. Both Larissa and Kayla stayed in the water for a moment, neither one wanting to exit the water for fear of ghosts.

"You think there are more out there?" Kayla asked with fear in her voice.

"There are," Larissa said looking around. "We need to be very careful. We both carry an EPD pistol and a Beretta in holsters while carrying the shotguns at the ready."

Larissa got the weapons out of the canoes and got onto land. She looked around and when she was sure it was safe, nodded to Kayla who got out of the water and joined her. They checked their weapons over and got them into position before scanning the area.

They were at a farmyard that was set against the river. Trees on three sides and the river on one surrounded the yard. There was only one path leading away from the farm and the rest was dense forest. In the yard, the grass was tall and green. There was a large, two story, square house and a smaller, one story, long house. Both were falling down. Four dilapidated barns were scattered around the yard, intermixed with corncribs and a granary. There was old, rusty farm machinery parked randomly around the yard.

"This site wasn't mentioned in Ethan's journal, was it?" Kayla asked.

"It wasn't," Larissa said. "As far as we could tell, no human has set foot here for fifty years, when the place was abandoned. There was a drought in the area and many farmers had to pack up and leave."

"Why didn't Ethan look here?" Kayla asked.

"Because he most likely didn't know about it," Larissa said, walking into the yard. "Michelle didn't either. There are many sites like this throughout the forest. The only reason we know about this one was the satellite imaging."

"What are we looking for?"

"Anything related to Ghost Town Labs," Larissa said getting closer to a barn where the door had fallen off. "We never heard from Hannah, Mackenzie, and Anna and we suspect that they came back. This place was near where Hannah and Mackenzie had entered the forest the first time they came in. Quiet and stay close to me."

Larissa and Kayla kept their shotguns at the ready as they entered the first barn. Inside the barn was older farm equipment, rusting and falling apart. There were two tractors, a combine, and pieces of equipment that Larissa and Kayla couldn't identify. They scanned the entire interior of the barn, but didn't find anything important.

They left that barn and moved towards the biggest barn in the yard. The walk-in door was stuck; Larissa kicked it in. The rotten wood crumbled away when her foot hit it. They slowly made their way into the barn and were horrified by what they saw. A grouping of ghosts, about ten of them, was huddled around something on the floor in the middle of the otherwise empty barn.

Larissa and Kayla wasted no time in firing as fast as they could. It took a few shots per ghost, but they were able to disperse them all. When the ghosts were gone and there was a mist hanging in the air they saw what the ghosts had been gathered around, Anna Jenson was lying on the middle of the floor in the barn. They rushed up to her and Larissa checked for a pulse. There was one there and Anna was barely breathing. She looked up at them.

"Are you angels?" Anna asked.

"No," Larissa said. "RAW Troopers sent in to figure out what the hell happened here."

"Hell's full," Anna said coughing. "So the spirits of all evil people are walking the earth."

"What about the innocent?" Kayla asked.

"There are no innocents," Anna said with a sneer. "Everything has gone to hell and the world is going to be at the mercy of Ghost Town Labs."

"Why do you say that?" Larissa asked. "What happened to you?"

"I tried to come back," Anna said. "I thought I knew something, but I had to be sure. Brian, my partner, was Ghost Town Labs. I thought something was wrong with the way he wanted to conduct business. I thought he seemed to be doing stupid and reckless things. I confirmed it, though. When we got out of the forest, Hannah and Mackenzie wanted to go back to New Church to get Ethan and the Tesla girls. I came with them, but I deserted them when we were in the forest. I don't know what happened to them, I didn't see them again."

"What happened to you then?" Larissa asked.

"I got lost in the forest," Anna said. "It was like the forest was playing tricks on me. I wandered for a couple hours before I was attacked and brought here. I've been on this floor since then, with those demons attacking me."

"Why did they keep you alive?" Larissa asked. "Why didn't they kill you?"

"I have no idea," Anna said. "We need to get into the lab though. There's an entrance not far from here, up river at a mill. I know the codes to get in."

"That path is blocked," Larissa said. "There are lots of ghosts watching the river."

"How did you make it past them?" Anna asked.

"We hid in the water," Kayla said. "And slipped past them in silence."

"We have to try," Anna said.

"Can you walk?" Larissa asked.

Anna nodded and tried to stand. Both Larissa and Kayla helped her up and it took a moment, but Anna was able to stand on her own and walk. She walked around the barn and then motioned for the women to follow her out into the yard. They left the barn and looked around in the bright daylight. Anna motioned to the canoes.

"We have to get to the mill," Anna said. "We can get past the ghosts again."

"What's in the mill?" Larissa asked. "Why is it so important?"

"That's the only entrance I know I can get in," Anna said. "We have to try."

"No," Larissa said. "I follow my orders."

"What?" Anna said confused. "We have to get back there. It's the only way we can stop them. You must see that. There's no other way."

"I don't think so," Larissa said raising her EPD shotgun at Anna. "I don't know how I was able to feel you, get a pulse off you, but you're a ghost."

"There are four classes of ghosts," Anna said. "Spirits are mindless and weak. Shadows know their dead and can fight. Apparitions are fierce, mean, and will kill. They can set traps and hunt. Phantoms on the other hand, are pure, concentrated, evil energy. All the negative emotions from humans are put into the phantom. That's what makes them so evil, so cunning."

"Either way, phantom," Larissa said. "You can be dispersed."

Chapter #16

"Let's get the hell out of here," Erin said, jumping off the Hummer and getting inside. "We don't have the fire power to combat all of them."

"Good idea," Kelly said. "Everybody in the truck."

All the women got into the Hummer and Kelly quickly took off. As the fires were being put out and brought under control, some of the ghosts were going back to the houses they were hiding in. The fire trucks were disappearing, but Kelly didn't want to wait to see how it would play out. She raced the truck down the old forest road, heading in the direction where Rachel had come from. It didn't take them long to get to the end of the road and see where Rachel had burned the police cars. Kelly stopped the Hummer and the group got out and looked over the damage that had happened there.

"I wonder how this went to hell," Brady asked. "It looks like there are four bodies in the cars."

"Ghosts must have shown up," Kelly said. "I wonder if Blake and Jake died along with those cops. Rachel must have been alone so she went to the farm site."

"She must have been trying to find us," Maria said, "but she ran into the group. What's the plan, Kelly?"

"We are going to wait here for a bit," Kelly said, looking at the main road to see if there were any cars coming. "Maybe a half hour. Let the situation cool down in Whiterock. Then we can go back in and continue the search."

"We're going back?" Erin asked.

"We have to," Maria said. "It's a good plan. We have to be in Whiterock. We must learn how they got those fire trucks. Can they just manifest things or is there something else behind it. Also, how did they put out the fire? We have to have answers to those questions."

"Right," Kelly said. "We post up here. Everyone on high alert."

The four women spent the next half hour in an extremely tense silence. They'd seen what the ghosts could do, how they could set traps, put out fires, and they knew that this area would be a congregating area. They only had to disperse four ghosts in the time that they were waiting, and when a half hour arrived, none of them wanted to admit it. Another thirty minutes passed before anyone said anything. It was Kelly who spoke softly as she got into the driver's seat of the Hummer, "Let's go."

Kelly drove very slowly back into Whiterock. She half expected to see the school rebuilt, but when they entered the town, the school, the church, and about five houses were burned to the ground. Kelly really prayed that no people died and that the fire destroyed some of the ghosts. Kelly slowly drove the Hummer around the town, looking for anything, anyone. As she drove down one of the gravel side streets, Kelly noticed faces in the upstairs window of one of the houses.

Kelly stopped the truck and looked again. There were people up there but she couldn't make out how many or what they were. The women got out of the truck; all looking at the window and seeing the faces look back at them. Kelly motioned to the faces to come out and after a moment, the faces disappeared from the window. It took a moment before four kids, two boys, two girls, came out of the house.

The kids were siblings, between the ages of about six and fifteen. The kids were dirty, dusty, in tattered play clothes and looking scared to death. They were grouped behind the eldest girl who was leading them. She was trying to be brave, but looked like she'd lost the urge to care. She looked strong, but starving. The youngest, the other girl, was crying. She had a death grip on her brother, not wanting to let him go. Maria approached the kids with her sword drawn. She tapped each one on the head, making sure they were human, before motioning to the others to lower their guns.

"Who are you?" Maria asked. "Do you know of any other survivors?"

"We don't know about anyone else," the girl said. "We've been hiding in grandma's house since the night the demon women came into town."

"Demon women?" Kelly asked.

"They were big," the girl said. "Wearing strange matching outfits. They shot everyone. We watched them through the window. Grandma had died a week earlier and we were playing in her house. Mom and dad didn't know we played there. We saw the soldiers trying to load people on the buses. Then the women came."

"They turned everyone into ghosts," Erin said. "They separated their souls from their bodies."

"We've seen those things around," the eldest boy said. "They come out much heavier at night. In the darkness, they play, party, and dance. It's like a game to them. Anybody outside at night dies, and then they come back."

"What are your names?" Maria asked.

"I'm Tina," the oldest girl said. "This is Frank, Kevin, and Amy. The Johnson's."

"Well, Tina," Kelly said, "we're military and we can help you."

"You don't look like military," Amy said. "More like hiking and party girls."

"We are, Amy," Kelly said. "I promise you that we are members of an elite military group known as RAW Troops. We have other people in the area and we can get you out of here. Erin and I will take you to the farm."

"Farm?" Frank asked.

"Victor Tesla," Maria said, "was the one who caused this to happen. We have a group at the farm. That's where a helicopter will land that can take you out."

"I hated his daughter Madison," Tina said. "She always beat me out for the lead place on the soccer team."

"She wasn't his daughter," Erin said. "It was a setup from the start. Please, we have to get you out of here. Get into the Hummer."

"You two get to the Lutheran Church," Kelly said to Maria and Brady as the kids got into the Hummer. "The Good Shepherd Lutheran Church on the old forest road. Get there and wait for us. Maria, you're the spot commander until we return."

"Orders understood, Commander," Maria said. "We'll wait for you."

Kelly nodded as she and Erin got into the Hummer. Maria and Brady started to run towards the church. Kelly sped the Hummer towards the edge of town, but a group of ghosts rushed onto the road. Kelly instinctively slammed on the brakes before she had time to comprehend what had moved in front of her. The truck wasn't able to stop before she realized what they were. Kelly slammed on the gas to plow through them, but as the ghosts passed through the Hummer, they killed everyone inside. The Hummer slowly crashed into a house as Maria and Brady watched in horror.

Maria took off running as fast as she could. Brady was right behind her but could barely keep up with Maria's long strides. The two women rushed to the church and when they reached the doors, they locked them. Maria and Brady quickly made their way into the sanctuary and sat down in one of the pews. They caught their breath before they started talking.

"Now what?" Brady asked.

"How should I know?" Maria asked.

"You're the spot commander," Brady said. "Kelly bestowed you with it before she left. You need to make the decisions now."

"We're in a church," Maria said. "Let's find the communion wine."

"We're not allowed to drink," Brady protested as Maria stood and walked towards the sacristy.

"What are you," Maria asked sarcastically, "my mother? I was drinking by the age of ten. It helps me think."

Maria took off and entered the sacristy, while Brady stayed in the pew. Brady was nervous, afraid. She realized that she'd never before in her life felt such fear. She had just watched half her team get destroyed in the blink of an eye—no warning, no protection. Brady didn't know what to do, but she knew that drinking wine would not solve anything. Maria exited the sacristy with a bottle of wine, wiping her mouth. She offered the bottle to Brady who turned it down at first, but then took a big swig.

"Drink," Maria said. "We need to think."

"Which is why," Brady said putting the bottle down, "we shouldn't drink."

"Don't be so tense," Maria said. "It will get you killed. Let's assess the situation. Half our team is dead, and they had most of the supplies. The faucets work, so we can get all the water we need. I'm sure there is some kind of food around here that would sustain us for a couple days, if needed. The teams should be flying in soon, so we need to be able to get to the farm, but we don't have the

Hummer. And I don't feel like removing the bodies from it."

"We could search for a car," Brady said. "There are vehicles around."

"We could," Maria said thinking. "But, I think we should go to the grain elevator."

"Why?"

"The reports from the FBI journal said that at both the mill and the grain elevator in Blackstone Hollow had doorways that could enter the Ghost Town Labs underground structure. We should investigate if there's another doorway here in town. Plus, the elevator also has big trucks; maybe we could find one that we could use to get to the farm."

"Okay," Brady said taking another swig of wine. "Let's go to the elevator."

Maria led the way with her EPD sword drawn, while Brady followed. Both women walked gingerly, quietly, so not to draw any attention to themselves. The elevator was only a few blocks away, but it only took a heartbeat for the ghosts to appear. Brady had never felt as alone as they walked along the gravel roads of Whiterock. She could feel the evil pulsating from the town itself; as if the whole area had been stripped of its soul and was now one of those demons.

They reached the elevator without incident, but both women felt that someone was watching them. They entered the main office and were glad to see a large, International grain truck was sitting on the scale. It looked like a monster truck to Brady, and she hoped that Maria could operate it because there wasn't a chance that she could.

"Know how to operate that truck?" Brady asked.

"International 9400 tractor stretched into a tri-axel grain truck," Maria said. "Could drive that in my sleep."

"How do you know what it is?" Brady asked.

"I studied the area," Maria said looking around. "Studied all the things about farm equipment and how to operate them. Follow me."

Maria led Brady down a flight stairs and into the basement. The basement was dank and dark. Its coolness felt refreshing on the sweltering day. The basement was lined on one side with file cabinets and the other side with electrical boxes.

On the far end was shelving with random boxes and equipment stacked on them. Strange looking machines and lots of pails and buckets were lying about, along with a corner full of shovels and brooms. In the back corner, hidden behind a mess of objects, Maria found the door to the lab, complete with the electronic lock.

"Damn," Maria said looking the lock over. "Erin and her computer could have gotten us into here."

"Do we know if the lab is safe?" Brady asked.

"As far as we know it is," Maria said. "I wish we could get in this way but we can't. At least we can report that it's here. Let's head back upstairs."

Maria led the way back up the stairs and into the main office area. The women looked around and all seemed quiet. Maria found the controls for the overhead doors and opened them up before going out and starting the truck. The truck started easy and sounded like a strong runner. Brady was about to exit the office and get into the truck when Maria came back into the office.

"The truck has air brakes," Maria said. "They lock on and need air to release. We have to let the truck run a few minutes to build up pressure."

Maria seemed hesitant as Brady nodded at the explanation. Maria suddenly seemed different for some reason, but Brady couldn't figure out what it was.

"Let me see your guns," Maria said, staring at Brady.

"Why?"

"I want to check them," Maria said taking her guns, sword, and knives and putting them on a counter. "We've been doing some shooting today and I want to make sure that everything is in working order."

"I can check my own guns," Brady said. "But thanks for offering."

Brady took both guns off the back of her shorts and set them on the counter. She started to take the Beretta apart, cleaning the different pieces of it as Maria did the same. They both had the real guns apart and were checking them over.

"Brady," Maria said matter of factly. "Would you be a doll and get me a bottle of Coca-Cola? The machines right there. Get something for yourself too."

"I don't have any money on me," Brady said.

"I don't think anybody is going to arrest you," Maria said. "For breaking the door and taking a couple bottles of soda pop, considering the situation."

Brady looked at Maria, figuring she was right, but wondering why she didn't do it herself. Brady took a heavy weight off the table and proceeded to smash the plastic window that protected the soda behind it. It took a few blows before there was a big enough gap to get some bottles out. Brady took out two bottles of Coca-Cola, handing one to Maria, opening the other for her.

Maria set her bottle on the counter and approached Brady. Brady was just finishing her first gulp of the soda when Maria decked Brady in the head. Brady dropped the bottle and tried to get into a defensive position, but Maria was relentless. Maria rained multiple blows onto

Brady's head, quickly, without a chance for her to cover up or brace for them. Brady fell to the floor, on all fours as Maria kicked her in the stomach then in the head. Brady was spread out on the floor, unable to get up.

"Please," Brady said begging. "Stop. What the hell is going on?"

Maria stopped and allowed Brady to get on all fours again. Maria said something in Russian, laughing. Maria got on Brady's back and placed her arms around Brady's head.

"Please," Brady begged.

"Ghost Town Labs," Maria said slyly. "Defenders of the future."

With that Maria twisted Brady's head as hard as she could, breaking her neck and killing her instantly. Brady's lifeless body slumped onto the floor while Maria went back and gathered her guns and weapons. Maria rushed out to the truck, got in, and took off. Maria realized that the truck was still loaded with grain so she couldn't accelerate quickly with it. Maria drove out of the town and headed towards the farm smiling. Her mission was partly over: one team down.

Maria turned the truck into the Tesla farmyard and brought it to a stop next to Rachel's Hummer. She looked around and saw movement in a barn with an open door. Maria got out of the truck and rushed to the barn, hoping, like the Gamma Ground Team, no one here would see through her.

Chapter #17

Kevin went in to kiss Sara, but then something happened that made his heart skip a beat. A panel in the floor started to rise, between him and his weapons. Before he knew what was going on, another woman was standing in the room, putting the panel back in place. She was stunningly beautiful, six-feet tall, flowing blonde hair, a black, spandex, one piece outfit with knee high boots, knee pads, elbow pads, and gloves, all black with blue trim. Kevin swallowed hard when he realized that there was a Ghost Town Labs symbol on her outfit. He also began to realize how power and big this woman was. She just smiled as she seductively walked towards him.

"Who the hell are you?" Kevin shouted.

"We don't need names," the woman said. "Unless we are deceiving someone who stands in our way. Someone like you, so you can call me Sara."

"You will never win," Kevin said. "Ghost Town Labs will never have victory."

"Oh, we will," the woman said. "You have no idea. Now, you're military with extensive training; it wouldn't be fun to simply shoot you."

The woman approached him squarely. Kevin felt intimidated standing in front of this woman. The woman got into a fighting stance and motioned Kevin to do the same. He complied, laughing. He quit laughing when she threw the first punch, a devastating blow that rung Kevin's bell. He stumbled backwards a couple steps, trying to regain himself, but she was on him, throwing punches at his head. Kevin got a couple steps back and then rushed her. He lifted her up and tried to slam her on the ground, but the woman got her arms around Kevin's neck and used his own momentum to slam his head onto the ground.

The woman quickly lifted her right kneepad up, exposing her knee, which she then slammed multiple times into Kevin's face. Blood was flowing from Kevin's nose as the woman put her kneepad back into place. The woman then went to punch Kevin again, but he moved, causing her hand to slam into the stone floor. The woman let out a scream as Kevin quickly got up and landed a kick to her face. The woman hit the ground and Kevin went after her, throwing some heavy blows to her head and body. The woman covered up, but when Kevin hesitated to switch positions, the woman landed a kick to the back of Kevin's head.

Kevin fell back and the woman got behind him and locked her arm around his neck as she wrapped her legs around his body. The woman scissored Kevin with her legs as she choked him with her arms. Kevin was struggling with all he had, but couldn't stop this woman. She bested him and she wasn't going to stop until he was dead. The woman didn't release her hold until well after Kevin had taken his last breath. When she let him go, Sara took a knife from her bag and cut Kevin's throat from ear to ear. The women looked over their kill.

"What do we know?" the fighting woman asked.

"They know enough," the other woman said. "Enough to be dangerous and enough to know that we should be killed on sight. The guns they have, the EPD, those things hurt like hell."

"You should have realized they would check you," the fighting woman said lifting up the panel that she'd entered the room through. "I told you they would. Well, no worries. Come up."

The women stepped away from the hole in the floor as two more women, dressed identical to the woman who'd just killed Kevin, came out of the floor. Both these women had pistols with them, and one of them gave another pistol to the woman who'd killed Kevin.

"I'd love to fight them all," the fighting woman said. "Kill them all hand to hand, but we don't have the time. Our spies indicate that they will be entering the lab soon and we have to have all the traps and surprises ready for them. Follow me; we'll catch them off guard. We have limited resources in the lab since Doctor Tesla order the others to leave."

"Do we really need to kill these guys?" one of the others asked. "He looked so easy to kill. They pose no threat to us."

"Alone no," Sara said, "but together they can be dangerous. There are a lot of other people in the area today, all heading for the lab. We need to thin down their numbers and make sure that only one or two survive the lab. They can then tell the world what's coming."

"When does the attack begin?"

"Soon," Sara said. "Doctor Tesla has a city picked out and they are making the final preparations to unleash a full scale Ghost Town Event. After the first event, which history will call the Genesis Event, no one will dare to stand in our way. Follow me; I'll be the bait for this."

Sara walked out of the room while the other women followed. They got outside the building and slowly looked around. They saw the group of guys fanned out, searching the grounds. Sara motioned the other women to stay back. She then stumbled out into the open, falling down and beginning to crawl on the ground while calling out in pain. Mike, Tim, and Gary instantly rushed towards her and the three other women shot them as they approached Sara.

Sara and one other woman stripped the men of all their weapons, ammunition, and supplies. The other two grabbed shovels and began to dig in the mass grave behind the church. One by one, Sara and the fighting women carried the bodies of the Delta Forest Team, including Kevin's, and they buried them in the mass grave. The women filled in the graves with dirt but placed no markers to indicate where the bodies were buried. Their names were not written on the mass markers on the edge of the grave. Two of the women gathered up the men's weapons and supplies and headed back into the building while Sara and the last woman looked around.

"You think more of them will come this way?" the fighting woman asked.

"I doubt it," Sara said. "These were supposed to be the best. Good thing we sabotaged the RAW Troops before they even started. This is why Doctor Tesla hates governments so much. Some bureaucrat sitting in a posh office has no idea what really goes on in actual combat. The best lie we told him, 'Don't tell them what they will be in for, they won't believe,' that was the best lie of all. The groups were completely unprepared for what they were going to encounter. Then we made sure that their training lacked in certain areas, the people could be manipulated, and my favorite, their outfits are completely impractical for the job, not only making it harder to perform, but also to be taken seriously when they say they are military."

"How many of our people are with the RAW Troops?"

"Three," Sara said as she started to walk back to the building they came through. "One of ours is the person who put the RAW Troops together. We had a hand in this from the start. Doctor Tesla made sure to cover his tracks very well. He has people in all levels of government.

Using our man in the FBI, I gave the order to send Ethan Drew out here while making sure to control the information he sent and received about Victor, Ghost Town Labs, and the project. Ethan's a good man but he was nowhere near ready for this. He was far too green to be given this case."

"You're pretty high up in the chain of command then," the fighting woman said. "Yet you're still pretty young. How did you get this position?"

"Because my real name is Morgan Tesla," she said. "I'm Victor's real daughter. The one those bastards didn't know about."

Chapter #18

"There's someone in the spire at the church," Kyrie said. "I saw movement up there."

Jade pinpointed her scope in that direction and saw movement, but couldn't get a good look at who was up there. It looked to her like it was Brady, but she couldn't be sure. They watched as buildings caught on fire as debris rained down from the sky. The fires were taking hold as Jade looked away. She couldn't watch, knowing that her friends were there and from New Church, there was no way she could help them. She knew that she had to find Dale as quickly as possible.

Jade motioned Kyrie to follow her and the girls made their way down the stairs. They got to the entrance of the church and looked carefully around. There was no movement at all and the temperature in the church seemed to be getting hotter. They entered the sanctuary and searched, but there was no sign of anyone. They walked outside and looked, standing on the steps, but didn't see anything.

"We need to go into the basement," Jade said, standing still. "If that's where you heard him, I'm sure he's still there."

"Then what are we waiting for?" Kyrie asked.

"I'm afraid," Jade said. "I'm afraid of what we'll find down there."

When Jade spoke the words, she realized just how scared she was. The thought of everything that had happened, of all that she had seen, it all was so foreign to her that she didn't know how to proceed. She knew that they had to enter the basement, but she didn't want to. Jade took a deep breath and turned to head to the stairwell. Kyrie followed closely, but at the top Jade stopped and looked down. She froze and didn't move.

Jade took a deep breath and finally started to move. Jade led the way as they slowly made their way down the stairs. Jade had a flashlight out and scanned the area when they reached the bottom. They moved further into the basement and saw Dale's lifeless body propped up against the wall next to Anna Tassel's casket. Jade gasped. She rushed to him and assessed his injuries. It was obvious that his neck had been broken, and that he taken a heavy blow to the throat.

"What do we do now?" Kyrie asked.

"I'm not sure," Jade said. "He was the spot commander for this team. It was just Dale and me here. I guess the standard operating procedures for this mission was that no one was supposed to be alone. Let's go back up to the spire. I have a phone in my bag and I'll call the Omega Team's tactical commander and see what she says."

The girls quickly made their way back up to the spire. When they got to the top they both looked, Jade with the scope, Kyrie with the binoculars, at Whiterock and the school. They were amazed that although the school and some other buildings had burned, the fires were out. Jade was certain that the fires would burn the town. Jade grabbed her phone and made the call to the tactical commander.

As Jade was on the phone, Kyrie scanned the forest with the binoculars. She knew these woods so well, having spent her life here. Kyrie still couldn't believe that her entire life had changed the way it did. She couldn't imagine what would happen to her now. There was just so much going on and all she wanted was some certainty as to what was next.

"We have a plan," Jade said hanging up her phone. "I'm to abandon my post here and get you to safety. We have no first-hand accounts of what happened, so they really want to speak to you. It's my job to get you to the Tesla farm. How good of a swimmer are you?"

"Swimmer?" Kyrie asked. "Why do we need to swim?"

"The quickest way to the farm," Jade said, "is to swim one of the rivers from here."

"No, it's not," Kyrie said. "That is a quick route, but if we walked one of the trails we could make it there faster. We'd have to walk through a stream for about a mile, but it would never be deeper than your knees."

"You know the route for sure?" Jade asked.

"Positive," Kyrie said. "We can be there in a couple hours max."

"Okay," Jade said. "They told me to leave the big gun here and someone else will be sent here to post out, one of the Theta Water members. He's almost as good of a shot at a long distance as I am. Come on."

Jade grabbed the duffel bag from the spire and led the way down the stairs. As they got to the base of the stairs, Jade scanned the area with her EPD pistol. There was no movement, no ghosts anywhere. They walked into the entryway as both girls had their guns at the ready. They exited the church and made their way through the graveyard. They got outside the graveyard fence, and Jade turned to look back at New Church. She hadn't seen any movement walking out, but as she looked back, she saw two women walking out of the church.

Jade and Kyrie were stunned silent. It was two Ghost Town Labs women; dressed in their combat gear, and they were walking confidently towards Jade and Kyrie. Both girls were frozen, as the other women got closer. Both women looked to be in their early thirties, both with shoulder length hair in ponytails, one a blonde, the other had black hair. They walked through the cemetery and up to Jade and Kyrie, who both had their guns drawn.

"Stop," Jade commanded. "Who are you?"

"Not ghosts," the blonde said. "Drop your weapons."

"What do you want?" Jade asked.

"To carry out our orders," the black-haired one said. "Now drop your weapons."

Jade and Kyrie looked at the women but they didn't lower their weapons. When the women got up to them, they wasted no time in using precision kicks to take the guns out of the girls hands and send the guns flying into the grass. In the blink of an eye, the black-haired girl had Kyrie pinned down on the ground.

"Let me up!" Kyrie screamed. "Get off me!"

"You are not part of the plan," the black-haired woman said. "You just need to watch and stay out of the way."

Jade tried to move towards Kyrie, but the blonde woman grabbed her and pushed her back and away. The woman moved into a fighting stance as Jade tried to keep her balance. The woman stalked in while Jade was trying to figure out what exactly was going on. She noticed the Ghost Town Labs symbol on the woman's outfit, but didn't know why they would be doing this.

The woman pounced in, tackling Jade and taking her down to the ground. Jade reacted by wildly swinging a clenched fist. She didn't have time to take aim, but as the woman tried to dodge it, the fist connected with her eye. The woman was stunned and Jade attempted to get up, but the woman grabbed Jade's baggy shirt. Jade quickly wiggled her way out of the shirt, standing, trying to kick the woman in the face. Jade's shoe connected. It wasn't a square hit, but it was enough to stun the woman.

Jade rushed in, taking the woman to the ground. She managed two solid blows to the woman's head before she threw Jade off. The woman scrambled to her feet and landed a heavy blow to Jade's head, knocking her off balance. The woman took Jade's shirt and quickly wrapped it around her throat, choking her. Jade struggled for air, but couldn't do anything—the shirt was being held too tight.

Jade fell to one knee, then both. The blonde woman held the shirt on Jade's throat until Jade couldn't even stay on her knees. Jade landed on the ground as Kyrie continued to struggle to get up, but the black-haired woman easily kept Kyrie on the ground. Just before Jade blacked out the blonde hair woman removed the shirt and let Jade gasp for air. The blonde woman jumped on Jade, holding her down to the ground, putting her face right in Jade's, their noses almost touching.

"You just got beat," the blonde woman said as Jade continued to gasp for air. "Do you acknowledge that we could have killed you with guns before you knew of our presence here?"

"Yes," Jade said gasping.

"Do you acknowledge," the blonde continued, "that we could have beaten and killed you at any point in this very short fight?"

"Yes," Jade said again. "What do you want?"

"This is what we were told to do," the blonde said. "We're following orders, just like you are. The question is do you know what side you're on? We're on the winning side."

"Not likely," Jade said. "You will never be successful."

"You have no idea," the black-haired woman said. "None."

With that, both women stood up. Without another word, they walked away, back toward New Church. The blonde woman kept Jade's shirt as they disappeared into the church. Kyrie rushed over and helped Jade up. Jade took a moment to gain her bearings as her breathing pattern returned to normal. They both rushed over and picked up their guns. They looked around, but there was nothing around.

"What was that?" Kyrie asked.

"I have no idea," Jade said. "I couldn't believe the strength of that woman."

"Same here," Kyrie said. "I was using everything I had to try to stand and it was like she wasn't even trying to hold me down."

"They were Ghost Town Labs," Jade said. "I bet they killed Dale. They work for Doctor Tesla. Come on, we need to get to the farm."

"You want this shirt back?" Kyrie asked.

"No," Jade said looking over what was left of her outfit. "It's so hot out anyway, I'll be fine in this. Lead the way to the farm."

"Okay," Kyrie said. "Follow me."

The girls quickly rushed into the forest. Both women had their pistols at the ready the entire time they ran. When they reached the stream, Jade took her shoes and socks off and placed them in her bag. They quickly ran through the stream with all manner of animals watching them.

When they reached the trail that led to the farm, Jade put her socks and shoes back on. They had been running for a long time, and both Jade and Kyrie were sweating heavily. The heat was getting more intense as the day wore on. Both girls drank from Jade's canteen as they rested a moment. Jade knew they had to keep moving, but she was so hot. She took her shoes and socks off again and quickly got in the water, and submerged herself in an attempt to cool down.

The water felt great. Jade climbed out, put her shoes back on, and they started running again. It didn't take long before they got to the farmyard. Jade was confused, seeing not only a military Hummer of the Omega team, but Rachel's Hummer and a strange looking grain truck. Jade scanned the yard, looking for anything that could indicate where people were at when she saw movement in one of the open barns. Jade and Kyrie rushed into the barn, happy that they were no longer alone.

Chapter #19

Larissa and Kayla open fired with their shotguns and unloaded the magazines, but it seemed to have no effect on Anna. Both women quickly switched to their pistols. They shot, but Anna retreated back out of their range and disappeared into the large house. Larissa and Kayla rushed to the boats and reloaded all their guns. They looked towards the house, but they didn't see anything there. Anna wasn't showing herself.

"What do we do now?" Kayla asked.

"We disperse her," Larissa said. "We have to take care of her. I don't know how in the world I was able to feel her, able to touch her. The only reason I realized she was a ghost was the way she was insisting on us going back. I had a bad feeling about it."

"Me too," Kayla said. "What's the plan? How do we go about this?"

"Follow me," Larissa said. "And if you see someone, fire. Don't wait to ask questions."

Larissa led the way towards the house. As they were getting closer, they could see faces in the broken out windows. Larissa didn't know how they would be able to disperse Anna. Especially given the amount of times they had already hit her, she didn't know how much it was going to take. They got to the doorway of the house and Larissa looked inside cautiously.

There were at least twenty ghosts loitering inside. Kayla raised her gun to fire, but Larissa motioned to stop. Larissa took off running towards one of the barns. They got into the barn and moved towards the center of the building.

"What happened to shooting?" Kayla asked.

"Far too many of them," Larissa said. "We need to burn the house down. There's hay here. Go to the canoe and into the bag. I brought matches with us. Get them and come back here. I'll cover you."

As Kayla took off running to the canoes, Larissa crouched down with her gun at the ready. Kayla swiftly made it to the canoe and rummaged through the bag. She found the matches and returned to Larissa.

"Good," Larissa said. "Take a handful of hay with you and slip around back, taking the long away around the back of the barns. I'll go out into the front and try to distract them so they don't see you. With as dry as the weather's been, the house should go up quickly. Once the fire's lit, we have to shoot anything that tries to leave. We must keep them inside so they disperse."

"Okay," Kayla said picking up a bucket and filling it with hay.

Kayla got the bucket full and rushed out of the barn, heading towards the house. Larissa walked confidently into the yard with her gun at the ready. As she looked at the house, she could see faces in the windows and she could feel their eyes on her. Larissa hoped they would be able to get rid of at least some of the ghosts with the fire. Larissa saw Kayla slip around to the backside of the house.

"Anna," Larissa called out. "Anna, where are you?"

"Right here," Anna said stepping into the doorway.

"When did they turn you?" Larissa asked. "When did you die?"

"After I split from the group," Anna said staying in the doorway. "It wasn't five minutes after I'd snuck away from Hannah and Mackenzie that I was killed. I wandered as a spirit for a bit before becoming a shadow."

"What are you talking about?" Larissa asked moving closer with her gun at the ready. "You mean you can go from one level to the next?"

"You have no idea," Anna said laughing. "All ghosts start out as spirits. The strong ones last long enough to become aware of their condition, a shadow. A shadow needs energy to feed on, to make it stronger. It needs souls; that's why we kill. The more souls a shadow feeds on, the stronger they become. Even if I killed you now, and took your soul, there would be a little left, a little I couldn't use, so you would be a spirit for a short time, thanks to the device."

"What device?" Larissa asked as she saw smoke starting to rise in the back of the house.

"There's a device in the lab," Anna said. "It serves two purposes. First, it keeps all the ghosts in its range. The device is feeding us, giving us power. Outside of the devices range, we wouldn't last long, maybe only minutes. Even with as powerful as I am, I would only last a quarter hour. The other purpose it serves is that anyone who dies here will be turned. It's all part of the experiment."

"Is Tesla still here?" Larissa asked.

"Yes," Anna said. "He's in the lab right now. Gathering data with his researchers."

"How many are in there?" Larissa asked stepping back as she saw Kayla getting away from the house. Flames were starting to rise in the house.

"Not important," Anna said. "You'll never make it there anyway."

"Then how does a shadow become an apparition then a phantom?" Larissa asked.

"An apparition is a shadow that has taken other shadows," Anna said. "Taken their energy and made it their own. It's survival of the fittest; humanity at its basic. Live or die, survive at any cost."

"Then what's a phantom?"

"A phantom," Anna said as the flames were starting to consume the house. "Is an apparition that has taken humans. Lots of humans."

"Who did you take?" Larissa asked.

"Doctor Tesla has brought people in," Anna said stepping forward out of the doorway. "From bigger cities. Homeless, runaways, people like that. Not very strong souls but get enough of them and the power grows."

"Why do you kill?" Larissa asked. "It has to be more than just survival of the fittest."

"It's human nature," Anna said. "One of our basic instincts is to compete with each other. The myth is that humans are good by nature. The fact of the matter is humans are weak, petty, violent, mean, and jealous. Hate is far more powerful than love. Very few people have more love in them than hate. The soul is the essence of the human. Devouring a human soul is like consuming pure, concentrated hate."

"You're wrong," Larissa shouted. "Humans are good. Humans do good things."

"Do they?" Anna said getting closer to Larissa. "Or our most humans just too scared and weak to act on the true human nature?"

Larissa opened fire on Anna, shooting as fast as she could. Kayla, from a distance, joined in. The house was on fire, a raging inferno, but luckily, no ghosts were leaving the house. All the ghosts they'd seen were dispersing in the fire. When the shotguns were empty, Larissa and Kayla started shooting with the pistols. When the EPD pistols were empty, Larissa pulled her Beretta and fire four shots, none of them having any effect on Anna.

"Is that all you have?" Anna asked laughing.

Anna rushed at Kayla, but when she reached her, Kayla pulled out a match and stuck it right as Anna was getting close to her. Kayla touched Anna with the match and Anna screamed out in pain and fell to the ground. Larissa ran to the barn and grabbed more hay. She rushed over to Anna and dumped the hay on her as Kayla lit another match as set the hay on fire. Anna screamed in pain, writhing on the ground under the fire. Larissa rushed to the boat and reloaded her guns. She got back to Anna and started shooting. This time it only took three shotguns blasts to disperse Anna. Larissa and Kayla breathed a sigh of relief.

"What do we do now?" Kayla asked. "She was so powerful."

"At least we know they can't deal with fire at all," Larissa said. "That's good to know. Burn the rest of the buildings, burn everything here. Once it's all on the ground, we take one canoe and get to the farm as fast as possible. We need to get this information to the troops."

Larissa and Kayla quickly went to the barn and grabbed more hay. They started lighting all the barns, houses, and granaries on fire. When everything was lit, they rushed back to the canoes. Larissa untied the second canoe and let it float down the river on its own. They got into the other canoe and watched for a moment longer before starting to paddle up the river as they heard an explosion rock the forest somewhere.

Larissa and Kayla paddled the canoe as fast as they could. They both left their shotguns on their laps and had their EPD pistols very close by. When they passed through the area they'd seen the ghosts before, there was nothing there. They had no trouble going past the mill. Larissa worried that they hadn't seen anyone or anything. She was prepared for trouble, but there was nothing there.

The women got to swimming hole, the closest river point to the farm, and they shored the canoes. They began to run towards the farm, but as they got on the trail in the forest, a group of ghosts blocked their way. They quickly started firing, but Kayla's gun jammed. Kayla took a couple steps back while she worked on her gun. Larissa finished off the ghosts that were left. After Larissa dispersed the last ghost she turned back to look at Kayla, who was still working on her jammed gun. Kayla got her gun working as a ghost came out of the woods and attacked her.

Larissa watched in horror as a younger man, in jeans and a t-shirt jumped from the woods and took Kayla down. Larissa shot at the man, and it took almost ten rounds from her pistol before he dispersed. Larissa slowly approached Kayla's body, but she could tell her partner was dead. Larissa waited for Kayla to turn then she instantly dispersed her. Larissa wasted no time in resuming her run to the farm. It didn't take long to get there and when she did, she saw a number of vehicles in the yard. She recognized some of RAW Troops vehicles, but there was a truck there she hadn't seen before. Larissa saw a barn with an open door and movement inside so she wasted no time in running to the barn.

Chapter #20

Omega Entrance Team

All was quiet in the Victor Tesla farmyard. Jeanie Kinze paced back and forth on the porch while she waited. The tactical commander for the RAW Troops on the Whiterock mission, Jeanie had seen military action on six continents. An assassin with over one hundred confirmed kills, most of them by her hands, nothing scared Jeanie. Orphaned at birth, spending her childhood bouncing from one foster home to the next, usually getting kicked out for fighting. Jeanie ran away and ended up on the streets before she was ten.

There wasn't a thing she hadn't done to stay alive, and seeing what life had in store for people like her, Jeanie got fake documents to get into the army when she was sixteen. Standing out from the start, and never backing down or allowing herself to be pushed around, Jeanie advanced fast, allowing her to be one of the first RAW Troops members. Soon after, she secured her tactical commander position.

Jeanie knew everything about the Whiterock Incident. She had read Ethan's journal hundreds of times, had scanned over thousands of documents relating to the area, read everything the government could get their hands on about Ghost Town Labs and Victor Tesla. Victor had people inside the government who destroyed most of the information that they had on him and the project, but Jeanie thought she knew enough to keep the team safe and obtain their objectives.

Jeanie looked at her watch again. She had been airlifted to the farm, getting there before daylight, and she was waiting for the rest of the Omega Entrance Team, who were driving in with a Hummer. She had selected two men to be at the farm with her, two men she trusted and had trained with for the past two years in the RAW program. She knew they were the real deal although she hadn't told them what they were in for.

Starting the day in full, black military fatigues and accessories, Jeanie had taken her shirt off in the intense heat of the morning, leaving just a black tank on top. Jeanie hated being hot and her long sleeved shirt was already soaked with sweat. Jeanie had two pistols clipped to the back of her pants, an EPD and a Beretta. She had a bag with her full of ammo, extra pistols, and knives of both regular make and EPD blades. Jeanie had an EPD shotgun slung on her back and a small pair of binoculars on a lanyard around her neck.

Jeanie scanned the yard as she paced before looking towards the house and seeing her reflection in a window. Although she was only five-foot eight-inches tall, she carried and projected herself to be much taller. Big, muscular arms, broad shoulders, ample chest, six pack abs, and legs like tree trucks, just looking at Jeanie people knew not to mess with her. Her dyed black hair was in two tight braids that stopped at the base of her neck. A narrow, thin face and very tan skin, Jeanie smiled at her beauty, knowing she could kill in the blink of an eye.

Jeanie continued to pace; she hated to be kept waiting. The men were supposed to have arrived over half an hour ago. The first thought that had crossed Jeanie's mind was that they'd deserted. She knew them well enough to know they hadn't done that and if they did, she knew that they knew she would hunt them down and kill them herself. Jeanie knew that something must have come up preventing them from making the set time.

Jeanie took the binoculars and scanned the farmyard and trees around the yard. She looked into the forest, trying to see if she could spot the New Church spire where Jade was, but she couldn't pick it out through the trees. She knew that Jade would be watching the farm throughout the day. Jeanie felt an extra level of comfort knowing that a hidden sniper had her back her today.

Jeanie paced faster. She was not a woman to sit still. Often times, when she was in the army, she would sneak off the base, go to the worst part of town, and get herself into a fight. There were a few times where she ended up in a hospital, but, most of the time, she got her frustrations out and the poor sap she picked out was on the ground or in the hospital themselves. Jeanie looked at her watch again and cussed, angry that no one was there yet. Jeanie had orders to not investigate any buildings or the house until her partners were there, and of all the things Jeanie was, she always followed orders to the letter on a mission, which is why she survived so many hot situations.

Jeanie scanned the yard, hoping to see a ghost. Jeanie wanted to see one, to have the experience alone. Jeanie often said that nothing could scare her. Considering what she'd been through, it wasn't surprising, but the thought of a ghost had her on edge.

Jeanie turned toward the yard and saw it. It was a small ghost, the form of a man, but nothing definite. It was relatively shapeless mist that moved through the yard randomly. Jeanie smiled as she grabbed her shotgun and moved off the porch and into the yard towards the form. Jeanie was ready to pull the trigger when the ghost took the form of a big man, older, in jeans and a flannel shirt. He was ready to work the land. Jeanie paused for a moment as the man started walking towards her. Jeanie took the shot and it took three rounds before the ghost dispersed in the air.

Jeanie took a deep breath, glad that she was able to survive the first ghost of the day. She knew that the ghosts were able to affect a person, but she hadn't felt anything strange. Jeanie looked around the yard, but didn't see any movement so she walked back to the porch. She leaned against the railing and looked at her watch again. She cussed again.

As Jeanie pondered what she would do if her partners didn't arrive, a black, military Hummer entered the yard and parked near the house. Getting out of the driver's door was Grant Kodiak, a six-foot-six giant of a man. He had short, messy, brown hair, clean shaven, well-muscled and an intensity about him that you could feel. Grant was a thirty-year-old military expert who looked ready to milk the cows. He wore cowboy boots, denim overalls, a sleeveless red flannel shirt, and a Stetson hat.

Getting out of the passenger seat was Lou Decker. Six-feet tall, well-muscled, bald and clean-shaven. Lou wore boots, dark blue jeans, and a white t-shirt that was a size too small. Jeanie smiled as the men walked up to her. She'd picked them because they were the most well rounded guys in the RAW Troops. They could handle any weapon, kill with their hands, were cool under fire, both highly intelligent, and she'd trained heavily with them.

"'Bout damn time you made it here," Jeanie called out. "I was worried I'd have to do all the killing here."

"You were worried," Grant said. "That we'd show up and you wouldn't get to kill all the marks." Grant and Lou got onto the porch and both gave Jeanie a hug.

"You didn't have to turn up the heat," Lou said. "It's blistering hot here."

"Tell me about it," Jeanie said. "Even when the sun was down, it was hot. I can't imagine how bad it will be inside the house and buildings. There's no air conditioning or fans."

"Seen any action today, Jeanie?" Grant asked.

"One," Jeanie said. "I was able to get him. I don't think Jade and Dale are at New Church yet. I was the first one flown in. Now tell me, why the hell are you guys late?"

"There was another meeting," Grant said. "About this situation. All information puts Victor in the lab. They don't think he left."

"We assumed that," Jeanie said. "How's that new information?"

"Victor might be looking at this as a training session," Lou said. "See how his troops do against the military. We are to use extreme caution moving forward."

"Planned on doing that anyway," Jeanie said. "What the hell are they so worried about?

We got the weapons and power to take this guy down. This will be an easy day for us."

"We can hope," Grant said. "What's our plan?"

"The house first," Jeanie said. "Shotguns at the ready. Let's move."

Jeanie led the way to the front door. She squared up to it, kicked it in, and slowly entered the Tesla house. The air inside was stale and sweltering hot. The windows to the south had their curtains open letting the sunlight and heat in, trapping it in the house. The sunlight illuminated the house allowing the team to see the dark red walls and the strange décor of the house. Grant walked in front of the freestanding Knight's armor while Jeanie and Lou looked at the wall painting that had haunted Ethan.

"I've wanted to see this picture since I read about it," Jeanie said. "I couldn't imagine it from Ethan's descriptions. It is wonderful though."

"This house should be burned," Grant said. "Can't you feel it?"

"Feel what?" Jeanie asked.

"Something...evil," Grant said.

"Keep it together solider," Jeanie said. "We've got a long day ahead of us. I don't want you losing your head and freaking out on me in the first building we investigate."

"I'm just saying," Grant said looking around. "I feel something here."

"And they say I'm the woman," Jeanie said with a laugh. "Pull your bootstraps up, Kodiak, and stay focused."

A stair creaked. The group turned and looked, aiming their guns at the staircase. It only took a moment, but two ghosts entered the room. Jeanie got both of them, firing before the men could figure out what was really going on. Both ghosts dispersed into clouds of mists. Jeanie quickly reloaded her shotgun before looking at the men, who were both stunned.

"That gentlemen was ghosts," Jeanie said.

"But we could see through them," Lou said.

"Yes," Jeanie replied, "because they were ghosts."

"Unreal," Grant said. "I know that something was strange here, but I still didn't believe. I guess seeing is believing."

"Just keep your wits about you, Kodiak," Jeanie said. "We have a long day ahead of us."

Jeanie walked into the kitchen. There was still fruit sitting on the counter, the pantry was full, as was the refrigerator. Jeanie took a can of Coca-Cola out, opened it, and chugged the can. She pulled out two more and offered them to Grant and Lou, but they declined. They opened all the cabinets and drawers, all the pantries and closets. Other than the massive amounts of food, they didn't find anything interesting.

Jeanie led the way out of the kitchen and down a flight of stairs, to the entrance to the lab. Jeanie tried to open the door, but it was locked. She assumed it would be and they would have to wait for the electronics expert to help out, but she had hoped to be able to see it for herself right away.

The group went back to the first floor of the house and investigated the rest of the floor, the master bedroom, sewing room, living room, and family room. They were all the same: dark red, eerie decorations, devoid of ghosts. Jeanie couldn't understand how anyone could want to live in the house as dark as it was inside. The medieval décor didn't help either, but she did love how big and open the house was.

Without finding anything on the first floor, Jeanie led the way up the stairs to the second floor. The hallways on the second floor were narrow and dark. The heat upstairs was almost unbearable. The group slowly made their way, Jeanie in the front and Grant in the rear. They walked to the end of the hallway where Jeanie opened and entered the door on the left side.

The group was in Madison's room. Teenage girl's clothes were spread all over the room. There was a teddy bear on the bed and an open diary was next to it. The walls were blue and bare, no posters, pictures, or decorations of any kind. Grant went to the bed and looked at the open pages of the diary.

"Don't you dare, Kodiak," Jeanie said slapping the diary out of his hands.

"What?" Grant asked.

"You don't read a girl's diary," Jeanie said.

"There could be information," Grant said. "We could learn something from it."

"I know," Jeanie said picking up the diary. "But you're not going to read it, I am."

"Cause you're the TC?" Lou asked.

"No," Jeanie said scanning the pages. "Because I'm a woman and it's a girl's diary."

Jeanie quickly scanned the pages. She found Madison's handwriting very pretty, very girly for the type of girl that Ethan had described. Jeanie could tell that Madison was going through some heavy transitions and although she had put on a very tough façade, Madison was scared about what was going on. There wasn't any information that really helped them, but there were some interesting things in the diary.

"Anything useful, Jeanie?" Grant asked.

"She had a crush on Ethan," Jeanie said. "From the first time she saw him she wanted to be with him. She can't explain why, but she mentions she tried to spend time with him to get him to notice her."

"Nothing spectacular," Grant said. "I read Ethan's journal. I think it was pretty obvious that she liked him."

"Yes," Jeanie said continuing to read. "She keeps a very detailed report about her workout routines and what she eats, how much soccer and basketball practice she got it, talks about how she wishes there was a swimming team at the school. Nothing helpful to us other than she hates how her dad treats the family and how she feels that he isn't a part of the family."

"Do you think she had any idea what her life really was?" Lou asked.

"No," Jeanie said. "She didn't know. I just wonder what happened to her. What happened to her and to Ethan and Michelle as well?" Jeanie tossed the diary back on the bed. "We need to keep looking."

The group went through all of the dresser drawers and the closets but didn't find anything useful. They left the room and went to the room across the hall. They entered the room and realized that it was Michelle's room. The room was painted a dark pink, and all the drapes and bedding matched. Michelle had a lot more knick-knacks on her shelves, and had pictures of her with friends displayed.

Michelle's room was very neat and well organized. Her clothes were properly put away and there was no clutter. The group went through all her drawers and closets, but they didn't find anything that was useful to them. They went through Ethan's room and the other spare rooms upstairs in the same fashion, but didn't find anything that they could use. They didn't meet with any other ghost either.

Jeanie led the group outside and into the middle of the yard. They scanned the yard and Jeanie scanned the forest with her binoculars. There was calm in the yard and the group couldn't hear any animals. The cattle were still in their pen, eating hay and grass that had been left there, but Jeanie noticed that some of the dairy cattle that hadn't been milked were looking very sickly, their udders bloated and infected.

Jeanie led the way into the largest machine shed first. They entered through a side walk-in door and scanned the shed. In the front of the shed was a Gleaner L3 combine next to a John Deere 8820 combine, both with headers for picking up swathed wheat attached. Behind the combines was a John Deere 4840 tractor with a grain cart attached to it. There were a number of older grain trucks behind the equipment. The combines had shields off as if they were being worked on when the incident happened.

"They were getting everything ready for wheat harvest," Grant said. "This is all older equipment, from the 1980's, but it looks to be in very good shape. They must have taken very good care of their equipment."

"Do you see any movement?" Jeanie asked. "Any movement inside the shed?" They scanned the area, looking underneath and above.

"No," Grant said. "There's no one else in here."

Jeanie motioned and they began to move forward through the shed. They stayed near the outer edge as they walked past the big equipment. They kept their guns at the ready, but they didn't see anything. They made it around the shed, back to the door they had entered through, and they exited the building.

The group made their way to the next building, the barn where Ethan talked about the kids boxing in. The group entered the barn and they all gasped. In the barn was a circle of teenagers, two of them boxing in the middle of the group. They were transparent and didn't even seem to notice or care that the three military personnel had entered the barn.

The trio raised their guns and began to fire. It only took one shot per ghost to disperse the kids in the circle. When they were gone, the two boys boxing stopped fighting and looked at the trio. They started to move towards them, but all three needed to reload their guns. They quickly reloaded and started firing. It took over four shots each to disperse the boys. When they quit firing a cloud of mist hung in the air of the barn.

"We're going to need more ammo if each barn is like that," Grant said.

"There can't be that many in each barn?" Lou asked. "Can there?"

"There could be more in each shed, Lou," Jeanie said. "Who knows how many there could be. We need to remember to keep our magazines full at all times. Follow me."

Jeanie rushed back to the Hummer and took out more ammunition. They reloaded their guns and restocked the supply of ammo they carried on them. Jeanie took a small backpack and loaded more ammunition into the pack. She gave the pack to Grant who slung it over his right shoulder as they made their way back to the buildings.

Jeanie slowly entered a different barn. Their nostrils were assaulted by the smell of manure and death. A number of milking cows stood in block fencing while three cows were already dead. The manure was piled up in the barn and the stench was almost unbearable. Jeanie looked upon the cattle with sad eyes. She pulled her Beretta out and went, one-by-one, shooting the cows in the head.

"What are you doing?" Lou screamed as Jeanie shot the first cow. "We have to set these cows free."

"That's what I'm doing," Jeanie said as she continued to kill the cows. "These cows are all dying. They need to be milked twice a day. Look at them; they're in extreme pain. This is the only humane thing we can do to them."

Lou shed a tear as Jeanie reloaded her gun and finished off the rest of the cattle. When she was done, she reloaded the gun again and looked over all the cows making sure that they were out of pain and dead. She put her Beretta away, took up her EPD shotgun, and waited. She signaled the others to do the same. It took a minute, but soon the cows were back, they had turned into ghosts. The group wasted no time in dispersing the ghost cows, each only needing one shot before they reloaded their guns.

"The animals turn too?" Grant asked. "What the hell is wrong with this place?"

"It's a theory one of our people had," Jeanie said. "They think that the separator is one way to make a ghost. They also believe that there is a device running in the forest somewhere that turns anything that dies into a ghost."

"That would be staggering," Lou said. "Think of the implications."

"What implications?" Grant asked.

"What it means, Kodiak," Jeanie said, "is that every human has a soul, a spirit that leaves the body when you die. It means that this spirit leaves after the body dies and goes somewhere, and this machine is keeping it here instead of letting it go where it wants to go."

"Where does a soul want to go?" Grant asked.

"I hope mine goes to heaven," Jeanie said, "but with everything I've done in my past, I don't know if I'd be on the list."

"You've always had a good heart," Lou said. "Just doing what you had to so you could survive."

"I hope they see it that way," Jeanie said. "I'll find that out when I die which I don't intend to do today. We need to keep moving."

The group finished searching the dairy barn and then moved to the smaller machine shed. The shed was full of haying and baling equipment—no ghosts. The trio moved from barn to barn without encountering another ghost.

Jeanie led the group into the granary, a shed with six compartments for holding grain, and there they met another group of ghosts. They wasted no time in firing, and it took about four shots per ghost. They dispersed the ghosts and reloaded. There was a mist hanging in the air as they left the shed.

The group finished looking in the sheds and barns before walking along the garden, tree lines, and patch of grass where more farm equipment was parked. Jeanie climbed on the cab of a truck and scanned the area with her binoculars but didn't see anything moving in the yard or surrounding area. They had searched the yard and had been in every building.

"What's the next move?" Grant asked. "Where do we go from here?"

"We get some more Cokes from the kitchen," Jeanie said. "Then go to the big barn, the one with the group of ghosts in it. We open the main doors so that when anyone enters the yard they know where we are at, and we wait there."

"Wait there?" Lou asked.

"Yes," Jeanie said. "We wait there. Those are the orders. We secured the farm and checked all the buildings. We are supposed to keep this yard secure and ready to receive the chopper when it arrives."

The group went back into the house, grabbed food and drinks from the kitchen, then returned to the barn and opened the doors. They past the next few hours sitting and talking, pacing around the barn, making hourly sweeps, and waiting. They saw a number of ghosts in the yard get dispersed by Jade's sniper gun, shooting from the New Church spire. It was mainly quiet until a Hummer tore into the yard.

The group saw Rachel Chance get out of the Hummer and look around. She was flustered and scared. Jeanie called over to her and Rachel ran to the group in the barn. They could tell she'd been through a lot in her time here.

"Rachel," Jeanie said. "What happened? Why did you leave your post?"

"Everything went to hell for me," Rachel said. "Blake and Jake were killed and turned into ghosts. Cops showed up and they were turned. I had to burn their bodies in the cop cars that there were. I have all the cop's weapons in the Hummer."

"Did you drive through Whiterock?" Grant asked. "What was going on in the town?"

"I didn't see anyone," Rachel said. "I didn't see anyone real that is. There were a lot of ghosts. I heard a report say that this farmyard was clean. Is that true?"

"Is now," Jeanie said. "We took out a number of ghosts and your sister has taken quite a few out."

"Have there been any new orders?" Rachel asked.

"Nothing that I've heard," Jeanie said. "I wasn't at the final meeting, so I don't even know all the people out here today. We have the farm secure, are doing random sweeps of the yard and buildings, and have a base set up here in the barn. You need anything?"

"Water," Rachel said. "It's so hot here I can hardly stand it."

"It is unusually warm here," Lou said handing her a bottle of water. "The temperature stays in the 80's and low 90's in July, not this 104 we're getting now."

"Any rate," Jeanie said. "Stay in the barn with us. The chopper should be here in a couple hours."

Rachel was so glad to have actually found a group to team up with. After her team had died, she'd feared the worst for all the teams and she didn't know what she would have done if there wouldn't have been anyone at the farm. Rachel stood in the barn with the others and waited for what was to come next.

It was about one hour, a phone call from Jade, and an explosion in town later before another member of the group arrived. The Omega team was confused at first, seeing a grain truck drive into the yard, but we relieved when Maria Diego got out. She rushed to the barn when she noticed the others inside.

"What happened?" Jeanie asked. "What was that explosion?"

"It all went to hell," Maria said, her Russian accent so thick they could hardly understand her. "Erin and I were trapped in the school. When we got out, we blew the building up. The ghosts were setting traps for us; they were trying to kill us. Everyone else in my team is dead. Kelly, Erin, and Brady. Ghosts took them all out. I barely made it out of that town with my life."

"You're safe here," Jeanie said. "Everything is safe here."

The team began their waiting game again. Jeanie started to check her phone, hoping that someone would sent her a message, letting her know an ETA for the chopper or how the other teams were doing. There was nothing though. No information, no messages. There were ghosts in the yard, but unlike before, Jade was no longer shooting them. Jeanie was taking them out from the barn. Rachel was worried that something had happened to her twin sister, even though she'd called and was on her way. Rachel thought Jade should have been to the farm by now. They were having troubles keeping Rachel calm when Jade and a girl, Jade dripping wet, the other dry, ran into the yard.

When Rachel saw her sister enter the yard she ran out of the barn and tried to hug her, but Rachel was running so fast that she knocked Jade over. Rachel laughed as she helped Jade up off the grass. The others were approaching them as Rachel started to talk.

"Jade," Rachel said happily. "What happened to you? I got so worried when you stopped hitting the ghosts in the yard."

"Something strange happened," Jade said. "We weren't alone in that church. There were two very strange women there, they killed Dale and attacked us. They could have killed us at any time, but for some reason they let us live."

"And who is this," Jeanie asked looking at Kyrie.

"I'm Kyrie Hamilton," Kyrie said and told the group her story. "That's how I got to New Church."

"You're safe with us," Jeanie said. "You have contact with any other group Jade?"

"No," Jade said. "I did see Theta Water Team, in a sense. I saw their canoes tied together, floating down a river, but no one was in them."

"No one in them?" Rachel asked.

"Yes," Jade replied. "They were empty. I didn't see any other group. No sign of Delta Forest Team."

"Okay," Jeanie said. "Everyone back in the barn. Kyrie, you'll have to wait with us until the chopper gets here."

"I have clothes in the Hummer," Rachel said. "If you want to change."

"It's too hot," Jade replied as they all started walking to the barn. "I'll stay in this. But I'd love it if you had some water in the barn."

They got to the barn and Jeanie gave Jade and Kyrie bottles of water. They discussed all the things that had happed at New Church while they waited. Everyone was amazed at the stories of Jade and the women she'd encountered at New Church. They all felt for Kyrie when she talked about what she'd seen that night when her world was destroyed. They were still talking when another woman ran into the yard, looked around, and then ran to the barn.

"Thank God I found you guys," Larissa said as she entered the barn. "Larissa Abercrombie, Theta Water Team. My team is dead."

"You're safe with us here," Jeanie said stepping forward.

"Oh my God," Larissa said when she saw Jeanie. "Jamie, I didn't know you were a RAW Trooper. When did you join up?"

"My name's Jeanie," Jeanie said confused as Larissa hugged her. Larissa pulled back. "I've never seen you before."

"What are you talking about?" Larissa said. "You're not Jamie Kurtz? You were my nemesis in the four hundred. I could never out swim you in junior high. Then your family left the area."

"I've never had a family," Jeanie said. "I've been an orphan my whole life. My name is Jeanie Kinze."

"My gosh," Larissa said. "You look just like Jamie, she left when we were fourteen; I guess it's a coincidence."

"What happened to your team?" Jeanie asked. "Where are they?"

Larissa told them everything. The betrayals, the ghosts they encountered, the classes of ghosts, and everything that happened at the mill. The group listened with intent as Larissa explained how Kayla almost made it and what happened to Anna. Larissa didn't skip on any of the details for the group.

"So no one has seen anything of Delta Forest Team?" Jeanie asked. No one had. "Then I guess we continue to wait. We stay here in the barn and wait for the chopper."

The group moved to various places around the barn, all with their guns at the ready. They waited and waited, allowing the minutes to blend into hours as the sun descended on the horizon. After two hours of silence, Larissa motioned to Rachel to exit the back of the barn with her.

"What is it?" Rachel asked as they got outside the barn.

"Something's wrong with Jeanie," Larissa said. "We were best friends when she was known as Jamie, and I mean best friends. We did everything together. I know it's her by the birthmark that's above her waistline, on her right kidney. She hated it and refused to wear a two-piece swimsuit because of it. She'd shown it to me at a sleepover."

"Why do you think she's lying?" Rachel asked.

"That's the thing," Larissa said. "Her family didn't leave, Jamie was kidnapped. There was a big search for her. The thing of it is, I remember that her dad worked as a researcher for the military."

"What are you saying?" Rachel asked.

"I don't know if we can trust her," Larissa said as someone cleared a throat behind her. Larissa turned to see Jeanie standing there.

"I don't know what you are thinking," Jeanie said getting right into Larissa's face. "But I lived in different orphanages until I was ten. I was bounced around because of fighting. I ran away when I was ten and was on the streets since. When you were having your first kiss, I was doing whatever I could to get a meal. I got papers to get into the military. When you were going to prom, I was in the desert, shooting anything that moved. I promise you, I'm not this Jamie you're thinking of."

"You have the same birthmark," Larissa said. "You look just like her plus you're the right age. There's too much to write it off."

"I'm not her," Jeanie said.

"You are," Larissa said. "I remember her eyes, your eyes. I got the feeling the instant I saw you."

"I remember my life," Jeanie said. "I have memories."

"And they have mind control," Rachel said. "And if your dad, your real dad, was a military researcher they may have taken you to ensure his loyalty."

"It can't be true," Jeanie said. "It can't be."

"Can you admit," Larissa asked, "that there's a chance it could be true?"

"I'll admit," Jeanie said, "that Ghost Town Labs has the power to do that, but not that they've done it to me."

"There could be others," Larissa said. "There could be other people here that are working for Ghost Town Labs. You could be a sleeper for them to destroy this group. There were others, we don't know who they could have gotten to."

"So what now?" Jeanie asked. "What if I am a sleeper?"

"All I ask, Jeanie," Larissa said, "is that I get to stick with you at all times. That way someone will be on you who knows what might happen. If you do turn on us, I'll be there to stop you, and try to get you to remember who you really are."

"I think you're looking for something that isn't there," Jeanie said. "But I'll agree to you pairing with me. You and Rachel, but don't tell anyone else. I mean no one."

"Okay," Larissa said.

"I agree to that," Rachel said.

"Good," Jeanie said. "Now let's get back in the barn."

The trio walked back into the barn where everyone was spread out and silent. No one wanted to say a word, not after the day that they had had. The heat was getting worse and the Alpha Strike Force should have gotten there. The sun was almost gone and they didn't want to be out after dark. It was hard enough fighting off the ghosts in the daytime. It was then that Jeanie's phone rang. She answered it and stepped outside the barn to speak. It was over five minutes before she came back.

"I've got some bad news," Jeanie said. "Alpha Strike Team isn't coming."

"Why the hell not?" Grant asked.

"There's been a lot of interesting activity in Fargo North Dakota," Jeanie said. "About eighty miles north of here. They are sending the rest of the RAW Troops to Fargo in case that's where the next incident takes place. They gave me a code."

"A code?" Jade asked. "For the lab? What about Kyrie?"

"She's coming with us," Jeanie said. "It's time for us to enter Ghost Town Labs' Whiterock facility."

The group followed in silence as Jeanie led them to the house, then down the stairs to the lab, down the stairs to Ghost Town Labs, down the stairs to Doctor Victor Tesla, down the stairs to hell.

About the Author

Leif J. Erickson was born and raised on a grain farm outside Wheaton, MN, just a stone's throw from White Rock, SD, which served as the inspiration for the Ghost Town series. From a very early age, Leif knew that he was going to be a farmer, just like his father and grandfather. As he grew up, Leif learned everything he could about farming, always riding in equipment with his dad and helping out wherever he could.

After Leif graduated high school he attended North Dakota State University in Fargo, North Dakota, where he achieved a BS in Agricultural Economics along with a minor in History. During his time in college, Leif networked with many other farmers from across North Dakota, South Dakota, and Minnesota, while advancing his knowledge in all aspects of agricultural. With a diploma in hand, Leif returned to the family farm and started his career as a farmer.

The first season was very successful and stood as a testament to the hard work and education that Leif had received. All signs pointed to a lifetime career as a farmer until a family tragedy struck and the family farm was dispersed. For the first time in his life, Leif didn't know what he wanted to pursue for a career.

Leif returned to Fargo, ND where he began his career as a stock and futures trader. It was during this time that he began to become serious about writing. With one computer watching the markets, Leif would be on the other, writing. Leif quickly realized though that Fargo wasn't the city or location that he wanted to make a home in. Less than one year since he moved there, Leif moved to Plymouth MN, in the Twins Cities area.

Continuing with the trading and writing, Leif began to learn everything that he could about writing, about storytelling, and about the hero's journey. Leif spent his spare time reading novels or books about writing. It was during his time in the Cities that Leif wrote many, many different stories, getting the outlines and first drafts finished. In the three years that Leif was in the Cities, he wrote the first draft for over fifty different stories.

Leif received information about a career opportunity that was back in his hometown of Wheaton so he returned to go to work for the local grain elevator. The work was hard and the days were long without much time for writing. Leif missed being able to write every day. He had so many more stories that he wanted to write. Being aggressive and a hard worker, Leif quickly moved up the ladder in the company and within six months he was in a management position.

Although Leif had met and dated many women when he was in the Twin Cities, it was in Wheaton where he met the new Science Teacher at his old High School and within fifteen months of meeting the pair were married at Good Shepherd Lutheran Church in Wheaton. Many have described the pair as absolutely made for each other, and they spend much of their time hiking in State Parks or canoeing the local lakes and rivers.

Being back in Wheaton, Leif used his free time to polish up and finish some of his stories. He got two stories to the point where he was satisfied to bring them to the marketplace and share them with others. Although he still works for the elevator, Leif looks forward to the day when he can write fulltime, offering more novels and screenplays to entertain and delight others.

During his life, Leif was always quick to be able to tell a story. He had an uncanny ability to quickly make up a story on the spot (sometimes to the dismay of parents and teachers) and to pull people into the story with wild characters, amazing locations, and fantastical storylines. Although Leif focuses on science fiction, he's written stories in many different genera's including mystery, horror, teen comedy, western, and even a little romance.

Throughout Leif's writings you can see traces of his farm life and his love of nature. Being an ecologist and former farmer, much of Leif's writings feature forests, lakes, and nature in general. Leif has always been interested in science and what's possible for the human race, pushing the envelope of technologies, and finding how far humans can go. Much of Leif's science fiction writing explores these themes and ideas.

When he's not writing, Leif and his wife Brittany can be found working on their goal of hiking in every State Park in Minnesota or on the lakes and rivers in a canoe. The pair have some big canoe adventures planned, and have already canoed, from end to end, big lakes such as Lake Traverse and Big Stone Lake. Every once in a while, Leif will pull out his old Disc Jockey system and play a dance as the 'Leif of the Party DJ Service.'

Leif has been influenced by many different writers and stories. His all-time favorite story is 'Sleepy Hollow' by Washington Irving, a story that Leif reads every Halloween. Other influences on his work are the 'Dune' series by Frank Herbert, 'The Lord of the Rings' by J.R.R. Tolkien, and anything related to the Arthurian Legend. Leif also enjoys many other authors such as Charles Dickens, Michael Crichton, John Steinbeck, Isaac Asimov, Neil Gaiman, and F. Scott Fitzgerald just to name a few. Thank you for checking out a book by Leif Erickson. Please visit his website at www.leiferricksonwriting.com and purchase the other books that Leif has written. They will take you on a journey that you will never forget...

www.ingramcontent.com/pod-product-compliance
Lightning Source LLC
Chambersburg PA
CBHW071147170626
46809CB00002B/801